MW01490873

Colony

Paul R. E. Jarvis

Copyright © 2020 Paul R. E. Jarvis
All rights reserved.
ISBN: 979-8-55-006795-6

1.

Since the dawn of time, humans have tried to make sense of the cosmos. For our ancestors, the celestial bodies were deities whose capricious nature controlled both life's cruelness and fortune. Now, more than any other time, living among the stars, perhaps even becoming gods, was no longer a dream, it was a goal.

'Today's the day,' Kelly Brown muttered to herself, focusing on her reflection in the mirror.

Her brown, shoulder-length hair hung limply, and the creases from the pillow still lined her face. Over the last few months, bags had formed under her eyes which made her look exhausted, almost ill. Like most things recently, her appearance had been neglected, and now, like her hair, she was beginning to fray around the edges. Sitting on the edge of the bed, she let out a wide-mouthed yawn, disturbing her husband.

'How do you feel?' Ryan asked, cocooned in the bedclothes, his eyes shut tightly.

'I thought I would be more excited,' she said,

taking a sip from the glass of water on the bedside table.

'How do you know what to expect? You're about to do something no-one has ever done before.'

'It feels like any other day,' she said, disappointed in herself for not being more enthusiastic. 'It's just another mission.'

Ryan shuffled behind her, his muscular arms enveloping her. The tattoo on his upper arm distorted in the mirror as he squeezed her. She hated the way it looked but had never been brave enough to tell him. 'Just wait, it will hit you soon,' he said. 'But you're going to be okay.' He kissed her neck gently.

'But what happens if we end up like.....' she paused nervously.

'Like what?' he asked, knowing what she was going to say. 'You mean, end up like the crew of the Erebus? That's not going to happen to you. They've fixed the problem.'

'You can't be sure of that. No one knows what happened to them.'

'It's going to be fine,' he reiterated calmly. 'You and your team have been through the simulator so many times. The disaster was a freak accident.'

'You're right,' she said, trying to sound upbeat. 'If it's my day to die, there's nothing I can do about it.'

'That's what I've always liked about you - your unrelenting optimism.'

She smiled sardonically before drifting back to her ruminations.

'It's going to be some time before I see you again. I'll really miss you.'

'There'll be plenty to keep you busy until I touch down. The time will fly by,' Ryan said, planting another long lingering kiss on her neck. 'Now, get in the shower, or you'll be late.'

She glanced at the clock, swore softly under her breath then hurried to the bathroom.

Kelly was no different from other astronauts in being very superstitious. The link between fate and the stars still manifested itself despite centuries of innovation. She refused to discuss the Erebus mission in case their bad luck chose to adopt her. Months of investigation had concluded a software glitch in the landing computer had caused the crash. Consequently, global experts had recommended slowing the race to Mars, but the Agency, driven by their investors, continued relentlessly.

Feeling conspicuous in her ceremonial uniform, Kelly hurried along a corridor lined with portraits of the 'pioneers;' those astronauts who had made the ultimate sacrifice in the interest of progress; some remembered, others long forgotten. Through the external glass wall, she could see a queue of cars waiting at the entrance to the base. Everyone, staff and contractors alike, had much to do over the next few hours to make this mission happen. Already late, she squeezed past the official photographer into the cramped room where her crew were waiting. They leapt to their feet as soon as they saw her and she greeted them with a wide grin before quickly waving them back into their seats. Across the room, she caught the eye of Kenwyn Traore, the mission's medic, giving him a wink and a friendly smile.

'Good luck,' the tall, dark-skinned African mouthed, the moment recorded by the photographer's camera.

'Can you leave us, please?' Kelly said sternly, more of an instruction than a question for the journalist.

After gathering his equipment, the photographer left, closing the door noisily behind him. Once confident they were alone, she sat facing her team with the back of the chair between her knees. 'How's everyone doing?' she asked, trying to sound casual.

'Honestly? I didn't sleep,' Anna said.

The others mumbled something similar.

'Don't worry. It will take us around eight months to get to Mars. So, there will be loads of time to catch up on your rest. You all know I'm not one for speeches, but soon we'll be strapped in and ready to go. Once the bird's flying and we're weightless, everything back home needs to be in balance. We're not going to be a team if someone's head is messed up by something back on Earth. We all have to get that kind of stuff tight before we launch. If any one of you has any issues, now is the time to bring it up.'

She made eye contact with each of them in turn, but no one looked way or said anything. Anna began pouring a colorless liquid from a bottle into six shot glasses.

'A toast,' she said in her Eastern European accent.

'What is it?' Mac asked with his aristocratic Scottish air, taking one from the table and sniffing it.

'Finest Russian Vodka,' the blonde Russian engineer replied, screwing the red cap back on. 'They say Mendeleev, the nineteenth-century chemist, approved the recipe himself.'

'I don't want it if it's that old,' he joked.

'Peasant!' she exclaimed with mock exasperation.

Tony looked at Kelly for approval, and she duly

nodded. Without invitation, the whole group stood, glasses in hand.

'For us, for all those who have gone before us, and those like us,' she said. 'Godspeed.'

'Godspeed,' they said in unison before downing the alcohol.

The Chairman of the Agency rapped on the door, interrupting their chatting.

'Hi everyone,' the former Austrian astronaut said with his usual suave sophistication. 'Before we go in front of the media, I'd like to say how proud I am of each of you. Today your names will be indelibly written in the books of history, and I wish I was coming with you. If you are anything like me, you're currently experiencing a mixture of excitement and terror. Try to remember two things: whatever happens, look after one another. When you're so far from home, the only people you can rely on are those sitting next to you. Secondly, respect your commander. Over the coming months, many difficult decisions will have to be made. Kelly's a fine astronaut and an excellent leader. She was hand-selected to lead this mission, and for you to be successful, she needs you to do your job well. Remember to listen to her instructions. You may not always agree with her, but you must follow her. Together there is nothing you can't do.'

Everyone nodded.

'Now, shall we go and meet the press?'

Applause erupted as they walked onto the stage in the giant auditorium. The Chairman stood behind a podium emblazoned with the Agency's insignia while the six crew members lined up behind him.

'Ladies and Gentlemen,' he began. 'Our hopes and dreams define us. The drive to seek beyond the things we know is what differentiates us from the animals. Today, we look to the heavens for our future, and we believe Mars will provide solutions to many of our world's current crises.' Knowing how to work an audience, he took a sip of water, pausing for dramatic effect. 'This is not our first mission to the Red Planet, but it is the first time in human history we will be founding a permanent colony on another celestial body. This marvelous crew will be putting their bodies on the line so humanity can stretch its boundaries for a more certain future. These six individuals, these pioneers, are stepping into the void, pushing themselves to the limit.'

Kelly flinched at his choice of words.

'Let me introduce you to the crew. Over on the far end, Commander Kelly Brown will lead the mission to Mars.'

She stepped forward and waved politely before falling back into line.

'Her background as a military pilot, and her expertise in project management, means the team and the colony will be in very safe hands.'

A cheer developed spontaneously accompanied by rapturous applause.

'Next, we have Dr Kenwyn Traore, from Cape Town, South Africa. The mission's physician. He'll be responsible for the crew's wellbeing and will set up a medical facility in preparation for the arrival of future colonists.'

The medic gave a broad, warm smile.

'Next to him is Professor Wai Xu, from Hong

Kong - a botanist tasked with establishing a sustainable food supply on Mars. Beside her is Lieutenant Tony Zaragosi from New York. He is the Assistant Commander with a specialist interest in construction and fabrication. He will be instrumental in the creation of the colony's infrastructure. Then, Dr Michael McDonald, our Robotics expert, all the way from Edinburgh, Scotland. Using remote-unmanned vehicles, Mac will explore the planet, giving us a better understanding of the Martian topography and searching for mineral deposits. Finally, over on the end, Anna Chernyakov, from Krasnodar, Russia. As a Nuclear and Electrical Engineer, Dr Chernyakov will maintain the ship's reactor and establish a solar energy farm to provide the settlement with power. Ladies and Gentlemen, I present to you the crew of the Aeolis,' the Chairman shouted into the microphone.

A massive cheer followed, the applause deafening, and confetti and balloons exploded from the ceiling.

'God protect you, and may your mission be more successful than we ever dreamt.'

After posing for several official photographs, they left the stage while the Chairman continued to address the audience.

'I can't believe he called us pioneers,' Kelly whispered to Tony when they were out of sight of the cameras.

'Such a bad choice of words,' he commented, shaking his head in disbelief.

Next, came the part of the day she had been dreading the most. Kelly had to say goodbye to Ryan. The day's meticulous schedule had allotted only five minutes for the astronauts to see their families one last time. He waited for her, perched on the edge of a desk in a small office.

'I'm so proud of you,' he said, embracing her. 'My beautiful wife commanding the mission to Mars.'

'It's a bit daunting if I'm honest,' she said, burying her head into his chest. 'We've prepared solidly for months, but now it's become real.'

'I thought you said it felt like any other day,'

'That all changed out there. The anticipation of the crowd hit me.'

'You can do this. Your crew are excellent. Having Tony as your number two will really help. He's a great guy.'

'It's the weight of everyone's expectation.'

Ryan hugged her, flexing his arms around her.

'We can still talk to each other,' he said, kissing away her tears. 'At least for the first few weeks.'

'It is not the same thing. It's hardly romantic having all our conversations recorded.'

Ryan would be CAPCOM for this mission, the astronaut who would communicate with the crew once they had exited Earth's atmosphere until they left broadcast range. A favorite of the Agency, he would be commanding the Discovery, the follow-up expedition, scheduled to depart later in this launch window. His task would be to escort a large group of colonists and scientists, as well as a vast quantity supplies, to begin the expansion phase of the colony's development.

'I'm going to miss you,' she said with tears rolling down her cheeks, staining Ryan's shirt.

'Me too, but think what you'll miss if you don't go. Anyway, we can send messages over the datalink.'

'You're right,' she said, wiping her eyes.

9

'It'll be tough hearing about you on the news and not being able to hold you.'

'I love you,' she said. 'More than anything.'

'I love you too. Next time we're together we'll be on Mars,' he said, trying to remain upbeat. 'Go out there, give your audience the launch they crave. Travel safely, don't take any risks and put your name in the history books.'

2.

Dressed in wine-colored flight suits, the crew stepped off the small minibus, and stared at their home for the next eight months.

'Beautiful, isn't she?' Tony said, shielding his eyes from the dazzling, winter sunshine.

'Yep, let's hope she flies as good as she looks,' Anna quipped nervously.

'Anyone else a little overawed?' Mac asked, his eyes not moving from the spacecraft.

'It's a strange feeling,' said Wai Xu, her bobbed, jet-black hair poking out from under her baseball cap. 'I don't feel worthy.'

'We're not worthy,' Kelly stated. 'We may be the ones going to Mars, but thousands of people have toiled relentlessly to get us to this point. Let's do them proud.'

The six of them squeezed into the narrow elevator at the base of the tower and commenced their rattling ascent. After an inordinate amount of time, the doors opened revealing a gleaming, white spacious room. The familiar faces of the crew chief and her assistant greeted them.

'Welcome,' the chief said. 'Things have just got real, it's time to suit up.'

Kelly forced the communications carrier assembly onto her head, the tight-fitting black and white hood worn inside their helmets which contained the headphones and microphone which would allow them to communicate during the flight. She caught sight of Tony removing a coin from his top pocket and kissing it dutifully. Kelly said nothing - they each had their own superstitions.

Once dressed in their exosuits and helmets, the technician swung open the door, allowing Kelly to lead the way across the walkway towards the Aeolis. Many storeys above the ground, she looked beyond the guard rails and saw for the first time the extent of the crowd which had gathered to watch the launch. Awestruck by the sheer number of people who had come to watch this historic event she waved at them. A distant, yet audible, roar erupted when they saw the commander high up on the gantry.

Inside the confined space of the capsule, a ring of seats adorned the walls, each surrounded by an array of screens. White panels with red edging covered the walls, and the floor, within the circle, contained a huge metal ring which the crew's feet would rest upon. They quickly took their designated seats; their knees almost touching as they faced each other. The only light came from the displays and whatever came through the solitary window and the open door. Once in position, Kelly tested the capsule's communications, her colleagues sounding off in turn. Satisfied the system was working, she gave her report to the Launch Control Centre, triggering the ominous sound of the cockpit door being sealed.

'Confinement complete and cabin pressurized,' the Crew Chief's voice crackled in the commander's headset from outside.

'Roger,' she said, her eyes adjusting to the brightness of the screens in the relative darkness.

The spacecraft vibrated briefly as the walkway retracted.

'Proceed with the pre-flight checks,' an anonymous voice instructed in her ear.

'Roger that,' she said, nodding at her number two.

They proceeded through the printed checklist, Kelly calling out a system and Tony checking its status.

'All systems are go,' she said.

'Countdown clock set to five minutes,' the voice inside her earpiece said.

'Roger. Confirm five minutes to launch.'

Kelly switched off her external microphone to speak to the crew through the internal intercom without the entire world hearing.

'Okay, stay calm. We've been through this more times in simulation than I care to remember,' she said, looking at each of them. 'We're only passengers, so sit back and enjoy the ride.' Giving a reassuring smile, she flicked the switch back on.

'Aeolis,' Launch Control said. 'Close and lock your visors. Initiating oxygen flow.'

The crew followed the instructions, dropping the tinted screens on their helmets.

'Confirming all ventilation systems are working with no unexpected errors,' Kenwyn announced after reviewing his display.

'Roger. Two minutes to launch.'

The world was watching. Media teams from almost every country had gathered to report on this momentous event. Behind the assorted press vehicles and minivans festooned with satellite dishes, an estimated half a million people waited patiently for the launch.

With ten seconds to go, the countdown began booming out from loudspeakers, the crowd shouting out each number. The main engines ignited at seven, causing the fuselage to lurch ferociously as the spacecraft fought against its restraints. On the cry of 'three,' the solid-fuel booster rockets, mounted on the side of the Aeolis, shuddered to life.

The immense force of the engines was finally unleashed, sending billowing clouds out on either side of its base. Around the world, the onlookers took a collective intake of breath as the spacecraft made its first, tentative steps towards the heavens.

'Aeolis is clear of the tower,' came the announcement. 'Launch Control standing down. We wish you safe travels and Godspeed on this historic mission to establish man's first colony on Mars.

3.

'Aeolis, this is Mission Control,' a new voice appearing in Kelly's earpiece. 'Responsibility is now with us. Comms check.'

'Receiving you loud and clear,' Kelly said, her voice heavy with vibrato.

'Initiating roll in preparation for booster release.'

'Roger that.'

The crew said nothing as they began the controlled rotation to bring the two boosters uppermost, the expression on their faces grim and uncomfortable. This was the moment the Space Shuttle Challenger had exploded several decades earlier, the disaster occurring due to a leak in a fuel line; thankfully, not a type used on the Aeolis. Nonetheless, she knew it would be weighing heavy on them.

Flicking off the external communications, 'It's going to get a whole lot quieter soon. It's all going to be fine,' she said gently.

'Prepare for throttle up,' Mission Control announced.

'Roger,' she said, moving the selector switch on her intercom with her thumb. 'Preparing for throttle up.'

The Aeolis' liquid-fuel engine increased its power, jolting them suddenly.

'Commencing countdown to booster release,' the anonymous voice called out. 'Five, four, three, two, one, release!'

The separation motors fired, pushing the giant thrusters away from the fuselage. The cacophonous juddering inside the cockpit disappeared instantly. The detached rockets continued on their upward trajectory, while the ship and its crew held a slightly lower course. The craft, now smaller, powered onwards as the separated rockets commenced their computer-controlled descent back towards the launch pad.

Three minutes later, they left Earth's atmosphere, only the white vapor trail now visible from the ground. The crew's bodies fought against their harnesses due to the sudden lack of gravity.

'Navigation computer has locked onto the target,' Kelly stated, spotting a light, high on the panel in front of her, turning from red to green.

'Roger. Telemetry showing the signal is strong, and the course is correct,' Mission Control acknowledged.

'Prepare to jettison the main engine.'

'Roger,' the commander said, the radio signal drifting temporarily.

The capsule detached with a soft judder, the body of the craft falling away.

'Separation complete,' Mission Control reported.

The tall rocket began its descent back to Earth

while the small remnant of the Aeolis continued under its own propulsion.

'Engaging docking computer,' announced Tony.

'Roger.'

Tiny bursts from the individual thrusters maneuvered the craft as the system adjusted their trajectory with pinpoint accuracy. In the cabin, everyone seemed relaxed apart from Tony, who focused intently on the screen in front of him.

A sustained burst from the retros, reduced their speed to almost zero.

'In five, four, three, two, one. Contact,' a specialist said over the intercom as the capsule shuddered as it slipped into position.

Several loud thuds followed as the anchoring bolts secured the Aeolis onto the front of the waiting cargo craft, prompting another light to change color on the panel in front of Kelly.

'Docking complete. All signs good,' Tony said into his microphone, looking up from his screen. 'Capsule is secured.'

They proceeded through yet another checklist, just as they had multiple times during simulations.

'All systems are green', Kelly announced into her headset.

'Roger that,' Mission Control acknowledged. 'Congratulations! It's safe to proceed with boarding.'

'Thank you,' she said, feeling immense relief.

Kelly unclicked her harness and immediately beginning to float. Using the grab bars, she pulled herself to the instrument panel on the wall, wanting to be certain the capsule and the cargo vessel were both pressurized adequately. According to the screen, air pressure, oxygen and carbon dioxide levels were optimal with no leaks. Relieved, she removed her helmet and took a deep breath.

Pulling herself across the room, she heaved the massive wheel in what had been the floor, where their feet had rested moments before. The door swung open slowly, revealing the interior of their new home. As they had rehearsed a thousand times, the crew drifted into the Communications Room.

The interior walls of the cargo ship were various hues of red and grey, lit by a mixture of LEDs and fluorescent tubes which changed color throughout the day in an attempt to maintain the crew's circadian rhythm. A team of psychologists had been used to finalize the color scheme, choosing a palate to provide calm reassurance for the crew during their journey into deep space.

'I never liked that cramped capsule,' Mac said, relieved to be able to stretch his long legs.

'It served a purpose,' Wai said with her usual emotionless tone.

'Wow! Look at that,' Anna exclaimed. 'That's amazing.'

They gathered around the door of the deactivated airlock, steadying themselves as they jostled to get a view of the distant Earth in the inky blackness of space.

'I don't think I'll ever get used to seeing that' Mac commented.

'Make the most of it,' Tony commented. 'It may be the last time we see it.'

'All right, settle down,' Kelly said, trying to control her movements. 'We're safely out of Earth's atmosphere, and this will be our home for the next few months. Check out your quarters, find where they've stowed your stuff then review your functional areas.'

'Hang on!' Kenwyn called out. 'Before you leave, can I remind you to do your daily sessions on the treadmill. Weightlessness leads to muscle wastage and the calcium leaching from your bones. Spending thirty minutes running each day will minimize this.'

'It is important,' Kelly added firmly. 'If we're going to build this colony, we'll need to stay strong.'

'The other piece of news I have,' he said wryly. 'You all need monthly injections to provide essential vitamins and to stimulate the production of blood cells. The first set of jabs is tonight.'

Everyone groaned.

'We've only just left Earth,' said Wai.' Why do we need vaccinations today?'

'Your bone marrow takes a hammering during space travel. The shots take a few months to work. If we start now, it will reduce the likelihood of anemia and infection.'

'But why didn't they give us them when we were back home?'

'There's a small risk of an adverse reaction, and the Agency didn't want the vaccinations to interfere with the launch.'

'What kind of adverse reactions?' Tony queried in his New York Italian accent, the concern in his voice betraying his calm exterior.

'Soreness at the injection site, a rash, that sort of thing,' the medic said. 'Nothing too serious, but I'll be watching all of you for any abnormal signs.'

'Right,' said Kelly, wrapping up the meeting. 'It's

vaccinations tonight and don't forget to do your daily exercise. In the meantime, please check your systems and let me know if anything is out of order.'

'Anna, can I have a word?' Kelly called as everyone began to move away.

'Of course, what's up?'

'Can you check the reactor's okay first? I want to make sure it wasn't damaged when this crate blasted off.'

'Sure. I don't anticipate any problems. The instruments are all showing readings in the normal range, but I'll give it the once over.'

'Aeolis, this is CAPCOM,' a familiar voice interrupted over the ship's communications system. 'Congratulations on your success so far. Can you give us a status report please?'

'Hi CAPCOM,' Kelly replied playfully, recognizing her husband's voice. 'We're undertaking a full systems check before proceeding to our course.'

'Roger that.'

The cargo ship had been launched from a Spaceport in Kazakhstan a couple of months earlier. These were always unmanned activities, primarily for safety reasons. Despite thousands of hours of preparation, launch still remained an inherently risky event. Unlike the Aeolis, it was powered by nuclear fission. Not only would it propel them towards Mars, but it would become the colony's temporary power supply until alternative sources of energy could be established on the planet's surface. A launch failure could result in a reactor breach, releasing a shower of radioactive debris which would kill everything within a hundred-mile radius, making the entire area uninhabitable for millennia. Consequently, ships containing nuclear reactors took off from remote facilities, far away from civilization. So, if there was a disaster, little would be lost, except for an unknown patch of land in the middle of nowhere.

Using the bars fixed at frequent intervals across the floor, Anna pulled herself down the Z-shaped corridor in the center of the ship, passing the crawl space to the upper deck before arriving at the reactor room. A yellow hazard warning sign adorned the door, informing everyone of the risk of radiation. On the wall, a meter showed the level of radioactivity was well within the expected limits. She typed in a code on the keypad, opening the control room door. Squeezing inside the tiny space, she fastened herself into the seat and began flicking through the various menus on the touchscreen. The current output was around five hundred thousand kilovolts, which is what she expected. She initiated the reactor's status protocol then sat back, waiting for it to complete a series of pre-defined tests.

Anna adjusted her hair, trying to add more volume after it had been flattened by her helmet. So far, everything was operating within normal limits. Importantly, the elevators which raised and lowered the boron control rods which adjusted the rate of energy production were working correctly. These occasionally caused issues with this type of reactor but were currently functioning satisfactorily. Finally, checks were run on the water levels, the efficiency of the turbine, and the reserve water pumps and, thankfully, the reactor had come through the launch unscathed.

Kelly stared out of the small window in her cabin, contemplating the journey ahead while her computer loaded for the first time in several weeks. Her bunk and the chair beside her desk both had belts so she could clip herself in and not float away. Unlike the other parts of the ship, their individual rooms were soundproofed, the Agency realizing the need to be truly isolated when confined with others for such a long period. Once the device had booted up, she opened the navigation interface. Scrolling through the list of nav beacons which had been planted throughout the solar system in the previous decade, she selected the final one, the Zipwire Beacon. This had been used by the myriad of drones and unmanned supply ships which had travelled from Earth to Mars, and now it would be their guide too.

Kelly held down a switch on the ship's intercom, 'The whole crew to meet in the Comms Room in five minutes please.'

She awkwardly made her way to the Communications Room where Tony and Wai were already deep in conversation.

'How do you like your new home?' Kelly asked as the others began to drift in.

'It's okay,' the assistant commander said. 'But I haven't seen room service yet.'

'I'm not sure it's that kind of establishment,' she smiled.

'I wanted to check the status of your functional areas,' she said once the full crew had gathered. Are there any issues?'

'I've been upstairs in the cargo bay. The

greenhouse panels survived take-off,' said Wai. 'I'll start to sow over the next few weeks.'

'Great, Thanks Wai,' Kelly said. Kenwyn?'

'I reviewed all your physiological data since we took off.'

'You've been spying on me?' Anna interrupted with mock outrage, causing everyone to snigger.

'Not exactly,' he said, becoming flustered. 'Anyway, no problems identified with anyone.'

'Good to know. Anna, how's the reactor?' Kelly asked, trying to get them all back on track.

'I put it through its paces, and it's not been affected by the launch. Everything is working as expected.'

'We can all breathe a sigh of relief then,' the commander said. 'Tony, how are the 3D printers and the fabrication plant?'

'One of the fabricators has been shaken out of position.'

'Is it still functional?' she asked.

'The restraining strap has snapped, but otherwise, it appears fine.'

'When will you be sure?' Kenwyn asked before Kelly had a chance to respond.

'It will be hard to tell until we've set it up,' Tony replied. 'But from the outside, it looks okay.'

'I'll have to let the Agency know,' Kelly said. 'If one of them is unable to function, there may be delays. Mac, anything to report?'

'Similar, I'm afraid. One of the drones shook loose during take-off. Its rotors have sheared off. It'll take me a couple of days to repair it, but nothing noteworthy.'

'Okay, a few minor mishaps, but everything seems

alright,' said Kelly. 'Let's get going.'

She floated across the desk, opening the communications channel.

'CAPCOM, this is Aeolis.'

'Go ahead, Commander,' Ryan's voice crackled through the ship's speaker system.

'All systems online and reading green.'

'Copy that,' Ryan said.

'We've locked onto the Zipwire Nav Beacon.'

'Roger. Go with ignition sequence.'

Kelly flicked through several screens, pressing the icon with some trepidation. After a few seconds delay, the lights in the Comms Room flickered momentarily as the craft's three engines drained power from the reactor.

'Sequence successful,' Kelly said. 'NavCom has control, and we are on course for Mars.'

'Good luck and Godspeed.'

'Roger that, CAPCOM. MYL, Aeolis out.'

Tony looked up from where he was sitting, 'What was the last message, MYL? I don't remember hearing that before.'

'Oh! Don't worry about that,' she smirked. 'It's complex commander speak.'

4.

A group of Australian high school students had sent a list of questions to the crew via the Agency. After weeks of travelling, messages from the Aeolis and Earth were now taking eighteen minutes to reach their destination. The delay meant they were no longer able to broadcast live from the ship, so Kelly decided to record her answers in the Comms Room, assisted by Tony, with Mac operating the camera.

'Do you have the questions?' Mac asked, bringing the shot into focus.

'Yes,' she said, holding up the cards.

'Tony, can you clip your microphone a little lower?' the tall, blond Scotsman asked. 'I'm getting some rustling from your collar every time you turn your head.'

The assistant commander moved the device down a couple of inches, 'Better?'

'Perfect. Good to go?'

They both nodded.

'Okay. In three, two, one,' Mac called in his soft,

flawless diction. 'Action'

'Hello, welcome to the Aeolis,' she started, self-consciously toying with her right ear lobe. 'My name is Commander Kelly Brown, I'm leading the mission, and this is Tony Zaragosi, my Assistant Commander.'

'Hello,' Tony said, smiling a little too excessively for the camera. 'This is a nice easy question to start with, how long will it take you to reach Mars?'

'It'll take us around eight months,' Kelly answered. 'So, we still have around twelve weeks to go. Okay, Tony, this one's for you,' she read from one of the cards, 'What's a launch window?'

'Ah! I need to explain a little. The distance between the Earth and Mars is not constant,' Tony explained. 'It varies considerably over time.'

'That's because they have elliptical orbits,' Kelly added. 'This means the planets orbit the Sun in an oval rather than a circle. Also, Mars takes twice as long as the Earth to revolve around the Sun.'

'We fly when the distance between the two planets is at its shortest, which, as we said earlier, is about eight months,' the short, Italian-American added. 'This route, known as a launch window, occurs every twenty-six months.'

Kelly waved for Mac to stop the filming.

'Everything alright?' he asked, turning off the camera.

She coughed then cleared her throat several times, 'I'm fine,' she said finally. 'Just had to cough.'

'Okay. Action!'

'So Tony, what's it like being weightless?'

'It's feels a little strange, but you quickly get used to it. As astronauts, we've all experienced weightlessness previously, like when we visit the space station. We pull ourselves around the ship using grab rails, but it takes a few days before you stop banging into the walls.

'The next question is on a similar topic. How do you go to the toilet while weightless?'

'That's a common question,' Kelly said, slightly embarrassed. 'We have something called a vacuum toilet. All I'll say is you've got to be careful.'

'Another one for you, Commander,' Tony said, reading the card in his hand.

'How does it feel to lead a mission like this?'

'I'm extremely humbled,' she said, contemplating her answer. 'Sometimes, it makes me sad there are not more women working in the sciences. I hope to be a role model for girls around the world. It doesn't matter who you are, if you have a dream, work at it. Don't let anyone tell you certain opportunities are closed to you because you're a woman.'

The session lasted for a further forty-five minutes, and the rest of it was recorded in a single take. After Tony and Kelly reviewed the footage and Mac's minimal editing, the movie file was relayed with a message back to the Agency.

'Thanks for helping with that,' she said, unclipping her microphone. 'Hopefully, those high school kids will be happy with the answers.'

'No worries,' said Tony, disappearing towards his quarters.

Kelly pulled herself out of the Comms Room, along the corridor to the Medical Bay. Unlike any other part of the ship, the room was brightly lit and the walls were covered in white ceramic tiles. Two beds surrounded by monitoring equipment occupied the center of the room and numerous cupboards lined the walls.

'Kenwyn?' she called, entering the room.

'Over here,' a voice bellowed from one of the small rooms off to the side.

'How are things here?'

'Okay,' he replied. 'There's so much to organize.'

'I know. Anyway, I've been wondering, have you noticed any issues with the crew's health?'

'Nothing which has shown up. Why? What's this about?'

'I'm worried about Tony. Something's not right.'

'How do you mean?'

'He hasn't seemed himself recently; I'm concerned he's spending all of his time on his own in his quarters.'

'I think he still talks to Wai a little,' he said. 'Being in space, this long can damage a person. Most people are aware it breaks your body, but it also messes with your mind. Boredom, anxiety, loneliness and claustrophobia are all demons which can haunt us. I can talk with him if you'd like.'

'Let me chat to him first, but keep an eye on how he's doing.'

'Will do.'

As part of the selection process for the Mars Program, the hopeful candidates had undergone an intensive simulation on an isolated mountain top in Peru. For three months, Kelly and five others had been locked inside a spacecraft similar to the Aeolis. During this time, they had no connection with the outside world, other than emails to and from Mission Control. Isolation had started well, with everyone laughing and joking, but with time, several of them began to isolate themselves from the others. Two of the crew developed overt neuroses and were removed from the program by the psychologists. By the end, only Kelly and Kenwyn remained unscathed. The rest of the Aeolis' crew members had experienced similar simulations, all successfully completing the confinement, and had progressed to be considered for this mission.

After taking a few seconds to compose herself, she tapped on the door of Tony's cabin.

'Come in,' he said, clipped on his bunk with a book in his hand.

'We've not really spoken for a while. How are you doing?'

'I'm okay. Just a little bored.'

'It won't be long until we reach Mars. Then we'll have lots to do.'

Tony said nothing but nodded slowly.

'You can always chat with me.'

'Thanks. Of the whole crew, I didn't think I'd be the one you would be having the "You're going nuts" talk with.'

'I don't think you're going nuts,' she replied gently. 'You've just gone a bit quiet on me, and we know the last quarter of the journey is going to be the toughest, so I just wanted to make sure you're okay. I'm going to need your help over the next few weeks.'

'I'll be fine.'

'Are you exercising?'

'Not as much as I should,' he said honestly.

'I need you firing on all cylinders when we land. We have a colony to build, and I can't do it without you.'

'I know you're right,' he said, loosening his tethering belt so he could swing his legs around to sit on the end of the bed. 'I don't know what's come over me these last few days. I'm lacking all motivation which is not like me.'

'Well, now we can do something about it,' she said sympathetically. 'I think you need more company. Try and engage with the rest of us a little more and talk to me if you notice you're drifting away, okay?'

'Thanks, boss.'

'That's what I'm here for.'

Wai, the shortest of the crew, had toiled for months in the small greenhouse area hidden away in the far corner of the cargo deck. It was not uncommon to see her slight frame, sitting next to her workbench, stooped over a series of pots. Row upon row of identical seed trays lined the wall in front of her, each cocooned in clear plastic boxes, designed to optimize the light and heat delivered from the banks of LEDs behind them. The site of the pale, green shoots emerging from the soil provided reward for the hours of work she had put in since they had left Earth. Beside her, several water-filled tanks containing the hazy blue-green algae, Spirulina, bubbled away.

'How are the tanks?' Kelly asked, making the botanist jump.

'They're excellent,' Wai replied. 'The algae's reproduction rate is at an optimal level, and they are producing more oxygen than we can utilize. They seem to be thriving.'

'I still can't believe this green sludge keeps us alive,'

the commander said.

'Don't forget we can eat it if we run out of food.'

'Hmmm! I hope things don't get that bad. It doesn't look all that palatable, does it? You're close to Tony, right?'

'We talk,' Wai replied, looking at images on the screen from her microscope.

'Is he okay? He's become withdrawn.'

'His role on this mission is construction. Unlike the rest of us, Tony and Mac haven't really got much to do until we land on the planet.'

'I know, but Mac's not isolating himself.'

'Don't worry. I suspect you're just seeing differences in personality type rather than anything being wrong with Tony.'

'Okay, but if there was a problem, you would tell me, wouldn't you?'

'Of course,' she smiled. 'I'm sure he'll be fine once we reach Mars.'

5.

After sending a message to Earth, Kelly hurried down the corridor, joining the rest of the crew for lunch.

'The NavCom says we'll rendezvous with Zipwire in a couple of hours,' she announced, taking her seat.

'We've made it!' Mac exclaimed. 'Brilliant. Well done, everyone.'

There were a few celebratory shouts from the others, but Tony barely reacted to the news.

'I need everyone to stay focused. We haven't landed yet,' Kelly cautioned. 'We'll remain in geostationary orbit overnight, so we can touch down at first light. There's a lot to do tomorrow.'

'Every second we're down there, Mars will try to kill us,' the assistant commander said finally. 'We've got to be careful.'

'Tony's right,' Kenwyn interjected. 'The Sun is a further fifty million miles away than it is on Earth. We're about to land on a frozen desert of rock, bombarded with cosmic rays. If the cold doesn't kill us, the radiation will. If that doesn't get us, then we have hypoxia to worry about.'

'We have to look after one another,' Kelly said, looking around the table. 'It's important we watch each other's backs. We have so much to do over the next few days, and the Aeolis will continue to be our home until the dome is deployed. Tony, your sole responsibility is to make it habitable. So, as soon as we're down, your job is to erect the dome then pressurize it. Okay?'

He nodded.

'Shouldn't we find water first?' Mac interrupted. 'It makes no sense if there's none nearby.'

'The Agency's geologists say the crater used to be an ancient lake. They're eighty percent sure there's water under the ground,' Kelly stated.

'So, that mean there's a twenty percent chance there isn't. It's a gamble.'

'I know, but the Agency say our priority is establishing the dome. If the area is dry, then we'll search further afield.'

He shook his head, unsatisfied.

'Mac, you'll need to go to the drop site and retrieve the Rover,' Tony said, trying to change the subject.

'Next, we'll need power and oxygen,' Kelly continued, regaining control of the conversation. 'Anna, I'll need you to connect the dome to Aeolis' power grid. It'll be a temporary fix until we can harness more environmentally friendly sources of energy.'

'Should be easy enough.'

'Wai, I want you to bring the chemical oxygen generators and the carbon dioxide scrubbers online so we can breathe the air inside without respirators,' said

Tony. 'Once finished, you and Mac can start building the greenhouses.'

'Sure.'

'I'll be setting up the water-recycling and the sanitation units with Kenwyn.'

'How long do we have to do all this?' Mac asked.

'Let's not rush, we don't want any mistakes, and we can't afford any injuries. But the sooner the dome is finished, the sooner we can move off the ship. Everything needs to be ready for the arrival of the Discovery. So, before we land, please can you check everything you're going to need for tomorrow.'

Over the next couple of hours, the crew prepared for the following day's activities. Wanting some time on her own, Kelly hid away on the upper deck of the cargo bay, in a dark corner next to the water recycling units. A strange tension existed amongst them. Other than Mac, who was always enthusiastic about everything, no one else expressed the levels of euphoria she had been expecting. Maybe they were anxious for what lay ahead. After all, the success rate for landing on the Martian surface was less than fifty percent.

From a list of hundreds of hopefuls, she had been chosen to be the first person to ever walk on Mars. Her name would be remembered throughout history. Amongst the mix of emotions, the specter of the last attempt to land on Mars still haunted her. She tried pushing it to the back of her mind, like a box neglected in the attic, but occasionally the lid would come off, releasing the fear held within.

'Here you are,' said Kenwyn.

'Hi, what's up?' she replied, leaving her ruminations behind.

'I'm checking you're okay. You have a big day tomorrow.'

'Yeah, the enormity of it has struck me,' Kelly said, aware the medic always knew the right thing to say.

'You'll be fine. We practiced this a thousand times,' his voice trailing off, noticing she looked worried. 'Are you thinking about the Erebus?'

'Don't ever say that again,' she snapped. It's bad luck.'

'Sorry,' he apologized. 'But I'm not sure me saying the name of a ship which crashed a couple of years ago will affect the success of our landing. They had a software glitch. We'll be protected by better programming, not superstition.'

'They were only meant to spend a few hours on the planet before flying home, but they never came back. We're trying to do something much more complex, yet the Agency has never successfully landed a man on the surface before. What if we're doing too much too soon?' she said, grappling with her emotions.

'It's horrible to say, but their deaths paid the price of exploration. Without them, we wouldn't have made it this far. I'm sure all the gremlins have been ironed out.'

'I hope so.'

'If anything, what happened to the Erebus is much less likely to happen to us. They will have been overly cautious with the software.'

'I know you're right. It was playing on my mind, that's all.'

'I meant to ask, how did your chat with Tony go?'

'He says he's bored, but there seems to be more to it. He's not been exercising and, if I'm honest, he's become even more reclusive.'

'To be fair, none of us have been particularly active for the last eight months. We're all going to struggle to some extent. Why don't I assess him and make sure he's ready for tomorrow?'

'What do we do if he's not?'

'Then we really do have a problem.'

***

'Right,' Kenwyn started. 'I'm going to run a protocol which will ramp up quite quickly. It is designed to put you through your paces. You ready?'

'Yep,' Tony said through the mouthpiece measuring his oxygen consumption.'

The treadmill began moving slowly,' and Tony, thick-set and short in stature with a Mediterranean complexion, started to shuffle along.

Over the next few minutes, Kenwyn cranked up the speed, simultaneously increasing the degree of incline. Tony kept up with the demand, but the medic noticed a distinct limp in his assistant commander's right leg. Tony looked in reasonable physical condition, but worryingly, he was consuming oxygen at a rate double what it should be.

'You're blowing pretty hard, Are you okay?' Kenwyn said, slowing it to walking pace.

'I'm fine. Just a little out of shape after this journey,' he replied, spitting out the mouthpiece.

Kelly's voice crackled across the intercom, 'I

wanted to let you fellas know, we're in orbit around Mars.'

'We've made it,' Tony said, more in relief than excitement.

'Yes, but now the real fun starts,' Kenwyn smiled.

He unclipped the harness, releasing Tony. The assistant commander winced as he grabbed the handrail above his head.

'Tony, what's going on?'

'I think I've pulled a muscle. It's nothing to worry about.'

6.

No-one slept particularly well as the Aeolis hung in geostationary orbit above the Red Planet. Someone using the noisy vacuum toilet adjacent to her cabin had been the final straw, but Kelly was determined today was going to be a success. In a crisp, new flight suit, she made her way to the Comms Room.

After clipping herself into her seat behind her desk, she stared through the airlock at the giant, red globe hanging in the blackness of space.

'I wonder what mysteries you have in store for us today,' she muttered to herself.

Like every morning, Kelly sent a video log to the Agency then recoded a private message for Ryan as live conversations had not been an option for many months.

One by one, the rest of the crew slowly joined her in the Communications Room.

'Today's the day,' Kelly said. 'Who's ready to make history?'

'Come on,' Kenwyn said exuberantly, speaking as

Tony was about to open his mouth. 'We can do this.'

'Get suited up,' she added. 'We've got a whole new world to discover.'

The exosuits had been specially created for moving around the surface of Mars. They were made from a lightweight polymer which shielded them from the harsh, external conditions, but light enough to allow them to move freely. The suits offered some protection from the higher levels of radiation they would be exposed to, but they would still have to limit their time outside. In addition, they would have to wear lead thyroid shields to protect the body's most susceptible part. Kelly hated wearing her tight exosuit, always feeling as if someone was trying to strangle her.

Through the visor on her helmet, she observed Tony going through his coin-kissing routine. He looked a little flushed, but she assumed, like her, he had also slept badly.

Once everyone had retaken their seats inside the capsule, Mac closed the door, turning the giant wheel, securing it in place. Tapping the blank screen in front of her, Kelly entered the passcode, bringing up a series of menus, her finger hovering over the drive icon.'

'Final systems check,' she said, each crew member calling out their status.

Everything was ready.

'Good luck,' Kelly said into her helmet's headset, before pressing the button. The retrorockets fired instantly, maneuvering the ship into its correct vector.

'Lower your tinted visors,' Kelly announced into her microphone. 'It's going to get lively.'

Soon, the smooth flight of the Aeolis became

incredibly bumpy. What started as a gentle hiss quickly became a jarring rumbling as they encountered the planet's atmosphere. Outside, the friction of their rapid descent produced flames around the small window.

'Temperature readings,' Kelly squawked into her mouthpiece, watching the usually calm Wai Xu grip the arms of her seat tightly.

'All within normal limits,' Mac replied after reviewing his screen. 'Heat shield is holding.'

'Roger that.'

Tony called out their decent velocities, trying hard to make himself heard over the increasing cabin noise.

'It's getting quite bright out there,' Anna said, seeing the flames out of the window.

'You certainly wouldn't want to be outside now,' Mac quipped.

The uncomfortable ride continued for many minutes until they entered the lower atmosphere. Suddenly, multiple parachutes deployed, causing the astronauts to lurch uncontrollably. The onboard computer fought to further reduce their speed, firing rockets to maneuver the craft.

Aeolis skimmed the Martian surface, heading for the Gusev Crater; the crew experiencing the unfamiliar sensation of gravity pulling them down into their seats.

'Atmospheric entry complete,' Tony informed them.

'Roger,' Kelly replied.

'Engaging landing computer,' he said.

'Thanks,' she acknowledged.

A low, metallic rumbling followed as four struts emerged from the fuselage. Once locked into position, a sustained burst from the small rocket in the belly of the ship slowed them until the downward velocity was zero. Aeolis hovered momentarily before entering a controlled, graceful descent. Finally, the craft landed on the crater's dusty floor.

'Touchdown,' Tony said.

'Disengage engine,' Kelly ordered, the relief in her voice palpable.

'Engines disengaged,' the assistant commander replied, looking up from his screen.

'Everyone, keep your focus,' the commander said. 'Systems check.'

Each crew member read out details from their screens, following the protocol precisely.

'Roger,' she said. 'All systems are green.'

Releasing huge sighs, their bodies visibly relaxed.

'What are our co-ordinates?' she asked.

'Fourteen and a half degrees south, a hundred and seventy-five east,' Mac said.

'Exactly where we planned. Welcome to Mars, everyone.'

'Way to go, Aeolis!' Mac shouted, slapping Wai, a reluctant recipient, around the shoulder.

Kelly smiled to herself. Every moment of her life so far had been leading to this moment. She opened the channel with Earth.

'Touchdown confirmed,' she announced.

Unclipping her harness, Kelly did not float away - Mars' reduced gravity was still enough to keep her

41

firmly in her seat. A refreshing change from the preceding months of weightlessness. The floor beneath her feet felt solid and reassuring, but her legs were surprisingly heavy as she tried to stand. She opened the giant door again, climbing through to the Comms Room where early morning sunlight streamed through the airlock window. They had made it.

Still in their exosuits, four of them crammed into the small space, while Tony and Kenwyn stayed onboard, watching through the glass. Agency directives dictated the assistant commander and one other crewmember should stay onboard when they first landed in case disaster struck. They had drawn lots and Kenwyn had lost, but he remained as magnanimous.

Slipping their tanks onto their backs, the four crewmates checked the power, oxygen and carbon dioxide levels on the gauges on their left arm in preparation for being the first humans to ever stand on Mars. Kelly pulled down the lever, gradually decompressing the airlock, waiting patiently until the light above the external door turned green.

Freed from eight-months of confinement, she gazed at the alien landscape, taking in the view. The yellow sky, contrasted by the dark, orange ground captivated her instantly. In the distance, the Columbia Hills on the crater's edge cast long shadows on the undulating floor, the scenery more vivid than any photograph could portray.

Steadying herself on the handrails, Kelly descended the steps in the landing strut, her legs unaccustomed to supporting her body weight, despite Martian gravity only being forty percent of that on Earth. Halfway down, she froze. What was she going to say?

Everyone remembered when Armstrong first walked on the moon; his immortal words had been straightforward, but perfect. She wanted to say something similarly memorable, but her mind was blank.

On the last step, she took a deep breath, preparing herself for what was about to happen. With the images captured on the Aeolis' cameras, Commander Kelly Brown stepped onto the dusty surface.

'These are the first steps on the road to creating Earth's first extra-terrestrial colony,' she said after a long pause, annoyed at how forgettable her words had been.

7.

Kelly stretched her arms out, spinning slowly, absorbing the unfamiliar features of their new home. The dry, barren wasteland, pockmarked by extinct volcanoes, spread as far as the horizon. Giant dunes of orange sand rose from the rocky surface, forming multiple ridges across the crater floor.

'Wow,' Mac gasped over the open channel. 'This is fabulous.'

'It's amazing,' said Kelly, pleased to have solid ground under her feet again.

Wai bent down and grabbed a handful of dirt, letting the red dust run through her fingers, 'We'll have to work this ground hard if we're ever going to grow anything here.'

'All in good time,' the commander said. 'Once the waste recycling units are online, we can start fertilizing the soil. That'll breathe some life into this.'

'I can't wait to explore the other side of those hills,' Mac said.

'What's it like down there?' Tony's voice appeared

in their ears.

'Amazing,' said Mac. 'Even better than I'd imagined.'

'Tony, you can suit up,' Kelly said. 'We're safe out here.'

'Roger that, I'll be right down.'

After allowing themselves a brief period of orientation, the eager crew commenced deploying the dome on the crater's surface. From the safety of the sealed control room, Mac opened the roof of Aeolis' giant cargo bay then expertly lowered the dome's metal baseplate onto the crater floor. As soon as the huge, metal sheet was unfolded and in position, the rest of the crew swarmed over it, bolting it to the ground.

Kelly watched with a sense of achievement as the reinforced, inflatable dome was unloaded. Large hooks were used to tether the structure in place before Tony connected it to a compressor aboard the spacecraft via a long, corrugated hose. Being on Mars exposed them to levels of radiation way beyond human tolerance. Consequently, despite their exosuits, they had to limit surface time. So, while the igloo-shaped dome inflated, they returned to the Aeolis, triumphantly celebrating their success.

'How does it look?' Kelly asked, handing Tony a cup of coffee.

'I still can't believe we're actually here,' he said, staring out through the glass. 'I feel like I'm dreaming.'

'Well, it's been a long time coming, but it's great to finally be here,' she said. 'It'll be hours before the dome's ready, why don't you have some food?'

'No thanks. I'm not really hungry.'

Re-energized, they returned to work. Mac began
lowering the prefabricated lead-lined panels for the
crew to secure onto the baseplate, enclosing the fully-
inflated dome. The whole structure had been
specifically designed to provide protection from the
rigors of the Martian environment.

Kelly and Anna discussed the best site to locate an
electrical junction box while Tony, Kenwyn and Wai
stood around, waiting for one of the gleaming white
panels to be lowered into place.

'Move it to your left slightly,' the assistant
commander instructed, the metal sheet swinging in
the air above him.

The crane whirred, as the peculiar-looking unit
inched closer.

'Hold it,' he said as Wai and Kelly locked the panel
into position. 'Okay, take it back,' he said, releasing
the crane's hook from the back of the structure.

'Only one more to go,' the commander said,
breathing heavily, unaccustomed to the exercise.

Tony continued to direct Mac when he suddenly
let out a grunt, collapsing backwards into the dirt.

'Tony!' Wai screamed, standing closest to him.
'Kenwyn, get over here.'

'Mac, stop!' Kelly shouted into her headset, the
large panel hanging ominously over their heads.

The medic ran to where his stricken crewmate lay.

'Tony, Tony,' he said. 'Talk to me.'

The collapsed man muttered something
incomprehensible as Kenwyn shook him.

'Let's get him to the Medical Bay.'

'Wai and Kenwyn, you two carry him back to the Aeolis,' Kelly ordered. 'Mac, Anna and I will secure this last panel in place.'

After pulling him up the steps, they laid Tony on the floor of the airlock before closing the external door. Wai knelt next to him, waiting impatiently for the room to re-pressurize. Even through his suit, it was clear Tony's breathing was fast and labored. Kenwyn stared impatiently at the internal light until it finally turned green. They hurriedly dragged Tony by the arms through the ship, heaving him roughly over the bulkheads. In the Medical Bay, they lifted their unconscious colleague onto one of the two beds, removing his helmet and unzipping his exosuit at the same time.

Apart from his shallow, rapid respirations, Tony lay motionless on the bed. Beads of perspiration gathered on his bald head; his sunken eyes glazed and unoccupied. Kenwyn slipped off his own suit, washed his hands, then examined his crewmate. A phlegmy rattle emanated from the back of Tony's throat with each rasping inhalation. Positioning a mask over the assistant commander's nose and mouth, Kenwyn set about listening to his patient's chest. Thankfully, the lungs sounded clear and his oxygen levels, displayed on the monitor next to him, were reassuring. Similarly, his heart appeared strong, but was beating with an accelerated rate.

The medic placed a hand on the ill man's abdomen which elicited a groan. Worryingly, the man's belly was rigid and tense; the slightest touch causing Tony to curl up his knees.

Kenwyn pressed firmly on the lower right portion

of the abdomen, making his patient cry out even louder.

Leaving the bedside, the medic opened the channel on the Aeolis' intercom, patching it into the crew's exosuits.

'Kelly, I need you back on Aeolis ASAP,' he spoke into the microphone with an uncharacteristic seriousness.

'On my way,' she said.

'Roger that,' he said, taking a seat in front of a computer.

'Anna, finish connecting the power. Just use temporary connections,' he heard her say. 'We can create more formal arrangements once all the other systems are in place.'

'Okay, boss.'

'Wai, are you free to come out here?' she continued. 'Now the dome's inflated, we need to get it pressurized. We can't do anything until that's done.'

'Okay,' Wai replied.

'Mac, unload the oxygen generators and the carbon dioxide scrubbers, please,' Kelly continued to give orders as she hurried to towards the spacecraft. 'Let's see if we can get them online before sundown. There's enough water on the Aeolis for the time being, so we don't have to worry about that, so let's focus on getting the air breathable inside the dome.'

'What do you think's wrong?' Kelly asked once they were alone in the Medical Bay's small office.

'It's almost certainly a perforated appendix,' he said glumly. 'Tony's abdomen is as rigid as a brick wall, and his blood pressure is in his boots.'

'Tell me straight, what's the bottom line?'

'If I don't operate, he's dead, but if I do, there's also a good chance he won't survive.'

'It looks like we have no choice,' she said. 'Let's prep him for surgery.'

Kelly arranged the instruments on sterilized, stainless-steel trays while Kenwyn inserted a needle into Tony's arm. The medic gave him a slug of antibiotics and a generous bolus of intravenous fluid. Tony put up little resistance, his naturally olive skin now a languid grey.

'Ready?'

'Yep, let's get this done.' the commander said, trying to hide her anxiety.

Kenwyn administered a hefty dose of ketamine, followed by a long-acting muscle relaxant. With Kelly performing the role of his assistant, he placed a tube through Tony's mouth into his windpipe then connected it to a mechanical ventilator. Happy with the position, they both scrubbed their hands in the small room next to the office then gowned up.

After prepping the abdomen with antiseptic, they draped Tony's body with broad, green sheets, leaving only a small window of skin visible.

Kenwyn picked up the scalpel tentatively, his hand visibly shaking.

'It's been several years since I've done this, and never on anyone I knew.'

'I have faith in you,' Kelly said with a reassuring smile. 'You can do this.'

The medic made a nervous, midline incision then quickly dissected down through the soft tissues; his confidence growing as he proceeded. As he cut through the peritoneal lining of the abdominal cavity, a horrendous, instantly recognizable, stench of feces filled the air.

'That confirms the diagnosis,' Kenwyn said, peering over his mask. Kelly nodded, her eyes betraying her calm exterior.

Using a vacuum suction device, he removed as much of the foul-smelling fluid from inside Tony's belly as he could.

'It's going to be touch and go. There's so much feces floating around in here.'

'He must have been ill for some time and kept it quiet.'

'Stupid idiot!' the medic muttered to himself.

Next, Kenwyn located the grossly swollen appendix. He tied off the angry-looking finger-like appendage before cutting it away from the healthy bowel. Happy he had removed the problem, and there was no further leak, he set about washing out the abdomen. He held the suction tube deep inside while Kelly poured in gallons of warmed saline, attempting to wash out the remaining contamination. Once satisfied there were no further leaks, he closed the different layers of the abdominal wall before Kelly placed a dressing over the surgical wound.

'Well done,' she said, helping him take off his gown.

'I hope he pulls through,' he said, extensive patches of sweat staining his green scrubs.

'There's nothing else you can do, it's down to him now.'

'I'm going to keep him asleep until his blood pressure is less volatile.'

'Makes sense. Stay with him,' Kelly said. 'The rest of us will do what we can. If things on the surface are delayed, it's not the end of the world. We can live in the Aeolis until everything is on line.'

'One other thing, I would like you to be my deputy while Tony's incapacitated. It's only a temporary transfer of command, but he's not going to be fit for a couple of weeks.'

'Of course,' he replied with a smile. 'But don't expect too much. I'm only a medic.'

'You'll be fine.'

Kelly made her way through to the Communications Room and slumped behind her desk, exhausted and emotional. A message from Mission Control waited for her.

'Congratulations on being the first people to walk on Mars. There have been huge celebrations around the world. You are now household names. Keep us informed of your progress. Well done commander.'

She had forgotten how momentous the day had been; Tony's collapse now overshadowed everything. Responding to the email, Kelly informed them about the surgery and the severity of his illness. She noticed a personal message in her inbox, presumably from Ryan, but she left it unopened. There did not seem to be anything to celebrate.

8.

The gradual droning of the re-pressurizing airlock dragged Kelly away from her thoughts. Shortly afterwards, Anna and Wai sauntered in, looking very proud of themselves.

'Radiation break,' Anna announced, unzipping her exosuit, letting it hang around her waist, exposing a white t-shirt underneath.

'Okay,' said Kelly. 'Give me a progress report.'

'Aeolis' reactor is connected to the dome,' the engineer said, removing her black and white hood and thyroid shield. 'We now have full power.'

'Excellent.'

'Mac has unloaded the oxygen generators and carbon dioxide scrubbers like you asked,' Wai said. 'We're waiting for it to fully pressurize before we can plumb them in.'

'Great work guys,' Kelly said with a forced smile.

'How's Tony?' Mac asked, joining them from the cargo bay's control room.

'It was a perforated appendix. The surgery went

well. Now, all we can do is wait.'

'That doesn't sound too good,' Anna commented grimly. 'He's going to pull through, isn't he?'

'To be honest, I don't know. Tony's very unwell,' she said candidly. 'But he's a fit, young guy, so his chances are as good as they can be.'

'He shall be in my prayers tonight,' said Anna.

'Well, he needs all the help he can get.'

'Imagine,' said Wai. 'Coming all this way and being struck down by appendicitis. It doesn't seem fair, does it?'

The four of them wandered through to the ship's small dining area next to the Medical Bay. Wai and Kelly took a seat on one of the benches as Anna rehydrated some food for them to share.

'The dome's looking impressive,' she said, joining them at the table. 'We're further on than I'd expected.'

'The pressure's at sixty-five percent,' Wai read off a tablet computer. 'We should be able to go inside in around an hour.'

'That's brilliant,' Kelly said, before taking another mouthful.

'We can't ditch the exosuits just yet,' Wai said. 'Not until the oxygen generators and carbon dioxide scrubbers are online.'

'Mac, once you've finished eating, can you offload the water recycling unit?' Kelly ordered. 'Then, while Anna and Wai plumb it in, we can go and find the Rover.'

'Of course,' he chirped. 'I'll do it now. I'm itching to get down on the surface.'

'This is where you're all hiding,' Kenwyn said,

entering the room. 'I thought you'd abandoned me.'

'Come and get some food. You must be exhausted,' said Anna, standing up from the table.

'Any more news on Tony?' Wai asked.

'Holding his own for the moment, but it's going to be a couple of days before we know whether he'll pull through.'

'Sounds pretty rough,' Mac said.

'Yeah, he's one sick puppy, but he's on optimal treatment so we'll wait and see.'

'Boss, where does this leave us?' asked Anna.

'How do you mean?'

'You know, with Tony being out of action. It'll be weeks before he's going to be fit again.'

'It's not ideal, but we know what needs to be done. We've all had the same training. We'll manage.'

'But Tony's the fabrication expert,' Wai protested. 'Without him, the greenhouses are going to be seriously behind schedule.'

'Look!' said Kelly, getting annoyed. 'We've all been trained on using the fabricators, so we'll have to make do.'

'Kelly's right,' Anna said, clearing away the food trays. 'We might not have Tony's expertise, but we can certainly make significant progress.'

'Anyway, it's time to suit up again,' the commander said. 'Now, let's get cracking. There's plenty of work to be getting on with.'

Kelly lingered as the two women left, waiting until she was alone in the Dining Room with Kenwyn.

'I wanted to say well done for earlier,' she said. 'It couldn't have been easy.'

'Thanks,' he said, slumping back in the chair. 'It was fairly stressful.'

'I thought you did excellently. I know you can't make any promises, but do you think he'll pull through?'

'It's not looking good,' he said, picking at what was on the tray in front of him. 'I would say no better than fifty-fifty. Tony's requiring maximal therapy to support his blood pressure. I'm worried the infection won't clear up.'

'Stay with him. We're ahead of schedule, despite you and Tony being unable to help with the deployment.'

'Sorry,' Kenwyn said apologetically, glancing at his tablet computer which displayed Tony's vital signs. 'There's so much to do.'

'Don't worry. We are where we are. Mac and I are off to get the Rover once he's unloaded the water recycling unit. For the next few days, your only job is to give Tony the best chance possible. Let me know when you need a rest, I'll sit with him.'

They heard the motor of the Aeolis' giant, robotic arms whirr into action as Mac moved the cumbersome unit down onto the planetary surface.

'When do you think we should transfer Tony into the dome?' Kelly asked.

'He's too unwell to go anywhere at the moment. Obviously, we'll need to set up the Infirmary first, and I'd like him to be awake before we move him,' he said.

'That isn't planned until next month,' she said. 'I guess it's become more of a priority now.'

'Not really. I can manage Tony's condition perfectly well here,' the medic said. 'There's no sense in moving him until he's stable.'

'Okay. the deadline will be when Aeolis has to return to Earth.'

Mac appeared in the doorway, now wearing his exosuit, his helmet by his side.

'Boss, you ready to go and get the Rover?'

'Yep, give me a few seconds, then I'll get kitted up.'

Sliding behind the desk in her cabin, Kelly clicked on the message from Ryan. A short video started, showing the deck of the Discovery. Her husband, surrounded by his crew, shouted their congratulations with streamers and spray string. The clip of the crew clowning around only lasted around thirty seconds, but it invoked a mixture of pride and homesickness. Once it had finished, she played it again, tears of joy collecting in her eyes. Despite the setbacks, they had made it.

***

'Do you want to do the honors?' Kelly asked, standing in the airlock.

'Of course,' Mac grinned.

He punched in the code then lowered the handle. The pressure decreased slowly until the light changed color.

'After you,' she said politely.

He descended the steps, taking in the new landscape, the dusty, rocky ground uneven beneath his feet.

'It's about a mile to the cargo site,' Kelly said. 'We'd better head off before the sun goes down, or we'll freeze out here.'

'Race you' Mac joked. 'But don't worry, I'll give you a head start.'

Prior to their launch, an unmanned, reusable freighter had delivered the equipment and supplies necessary for the initial colonization. The smaller ship was faster than the Aeolis and had dropped its cargo onto the surface in preparation for their arrival. Mac was particularly excited as one of the pods included the Rover, a six-wheeled vehicle designed specifically for navigating the uneven terrain.

Despite their best efforts, the hike quickly sapped their energy, forcing them to stop multiple times. Eight months of space travel had dramatically reduced the muscle mass in their legs and they had rapidly become exhausted.

'I think I can see them,' Mac said excitedly, pointing into the distance.

Kelly squinted for a few seconds then nodded. 'Not long now,' she said, quickening her pace.

The early evening sun glinted off the three white, metal pods which lay partially submerged in red sand. It was evident the fall from low orbit had not damaged them, hopefully the contents were also intact. Mac ran among the containers, checking the stainless-steel manifests on the door which listed the contents.

'This one,' he shouted like an excited schoolboy.

Together, they forced the giant locking bar upwards. The corrugated steel door swung open with a high-pitched grating noise, making Kelly shudder, then set to work releasing the supporting straps which had protected the vehicle during transit.

'Let's fire this baby up,' Mac said eagerly.

He opened the door at the rear, then squeezed inside. Making his way between the two benches running the length of the interior, he settled into the cab. The dashboard illuminated as he tapped in his passcode. Despite months of inactivity, the dial showed the batteries remained eighty percent charged. He pressed the start button, and after several coughs, the engine burst into life, prompting him to slam his fist down in celebration.

Once on the planet's surface, Mac punched the throttle, driving in a succession of widening circles. Listening to his squeals of joy in her earpiece, Kelly could see her colleague's broad grin through the plexiglass of the cab as the lumbering, white vehicle threw up thick clouds of dust.

'Mac, we haven't got time for this,' she said, after letting him enjoy a few moments of excitement.

'Killjoy,' he replied, finally reversing the Rover up to the second cargo pod.

Inside was a giant trailer, containing supplies and equipment. After removing the safety straps, Kelly hitched it to the vehicle.

'Let's go. With a bit of luck, we could come back and empty the third pod before nightfall.'

The underpowered engine caused the wheels to spin as they struggled to gain traction on the dusty crater floor. Nonetheless, Mac was jubilant as he could now claim he was the first person ever to drive on Mars.

'It's funny thinking this is going to be our forever home,' he said as the Rover lurched down a slight depression.

'I know what you mean. At the moment It feels like we're only visiting.

'Do you think you and Ryan will start a family here?'

'The medics back at the Agency told me we shouldn't try and have kids. You know, with all the radiation.'

'What about you?'

'I wasn't planning on starting a family with Ryan,' Mac smiled.

'No, I could see how that would be a problem,' she giggled. 'Do you want children one day?'

'I had never thought about it,' he answered honestly. 'Being one of the first people on Mars was too much of an opportunity to turn down.'

'I guess it'll be different when we start tunneling. Once we've built rooms underground, away from the surface radiation, maybe. But there's still a risk from all this exposure.'

When they arrived back at the Aeolis, Kelly was pleased to see the construction of the dome had been progressing nicely. The walls were in place, and through the window of the airlock she could see Anna, working without a helmet or an exosuit. In just one day, even after what had happened to Tony, they had created somewhere habitable.

'Should we go back to unload the third pod, Boss?' he asked as they unhitched the trailer.

'If we're doing it, we must go now,' she said flatly. 'There's not much daylight left.'

Mac jumped back in the cab and restarted the engine. Without its trailer, the Rover handled much better as they began their journey back to the pods.

Looking through the windshield, the crescentic

ridges of sand now cast long, dark shadows. The heavens had changed from yellow to a deep crimson, punctuated by Mars' two moons.

'Look at that,' she said, witnessing her first Martian twilight.

'That's something else,' he commented, gazing out of the window. 'It seems so strange having two moons. They don't look real.'

By the time they had arrived at the cargo site, the sun had disappeared behind the hills. The thermometer on the dashboard showed the outside temperature had plummeted.

'It's minus one hundred and thirty degrees,' Mac said incredulously. 'Soon it will be beyond the tolerance of our exosuits.'

Kelly was furious with herself. Realistically, by the time they got back to the Aeolis, it would be too cold for them to leave the Rover.

'Damn it,' she exclaimed angrily. 'We're going to have to spend the night here.'

'We could park inside one of the empty cargo pods,' he said helpfully. 'It'll give us some shelter. At least we have climate control, but it's not going to be comfortable.'

'I don't see many other options,' Kelly reflected. 'How are the batteries holding out?'

'Over sixty percent remaining,' he replied. 'We can't have tropical temperatures, but we'll be okay.'

Sealing the Scotsman inside the cab, Kelly replaced her helmet and exited through the rear of the vehicle. As soon as she stepped on to the surface, the temperature alarm on her suit started chirping.

'It's so cold out here,' she said, holding the pod's door open.

'Don't worry, this shouldn't take too long.'

Mac edged the Rover forward, stopping inches from the wall inside the pod. She closed the giant door behind them, locking in place before squeezing through the back door of the vehicle.

Once the cab was re-pressurized, they both removed their helmets. Siting in the passenger seat with her boots on the dashboard, she clicked the broadcast button on the Rover's radio, 'Aeolis, this is Kelly.'

After a few seconds, a faint, but familiar voice crackled through the speakers on the console.

'Go ahead, Kelly. It's Kenwyn.'

'We've run into a small snag.'

'What's happened?' the medic's voice heavy with concern. 'Are you two okay?'

'We're fine. We've just been stupid. It got dark much quicker than we anticipated. Now it's too cold for us to get back to the Aeolis.'

'What are you going to do?'

'We're going to spend the night in the Rover. We've parked inside one of the cargo pods. We'll try to be back at first light tomorrow.'

'Okay, but it doesn't sound like much fun,' his voice sounding tinny over the speaker.

'I can confirm that,' she said, her voice laced with sarcasm.

'I have some news which will cheer you up.'

'What?' she said sternly, not in the mood for games.

'The dome is now pressurized, and the pressure is holding. We have breathable air, but the Aeolis is supplying it with power and water. Unfortunately, there's no heating or waste recycling yet, so we can't move in tonight. Anna and Wai are now safely back on board the ship.'

'They must be exhausted. Say a huge thank you from me,' she said. 'How's Tony?'

'Much the same. He still requires inotropes to support his blood pressure. I've not tried to wake him yet.'

'If anything changes, let me know straight away. I can't imagine I'll sleep much cooped up in this cramped space.'

'I will do. You and Mac try and have a good night and stay safe.'

'Thanks, Kenwyn. Kelly out.'

'Sounds like they're making progress,' Mac said, trying to focus on the positives.

'Much better than I expected,' she admitted. 'I'm so furious about having to spend the night here. I could kick myself.'

'No harm done. At least we're safe, but it's going to be a long, cold one. To save power I'll only pressurize the cab, then we should have enough to last through the night and be able to drive back to the Aeolis in the morning. The cabin temperature needs to be no more than six degrees,' he said, staring at the computer's calculation displayed on the console.

'Six degrees it is then.'

'You'd think they'd make these seats recline, wouldn't you?'

'I'm not sure the designers had envisioned us using it for a sleepover,' she said with a resigned smile.

Mac dimmed the Rover's interior lighting, the two of them sitting and chatting in near darkness. Over the next few hours, moonlight began to filter through a small pressure vent high in the wall of the cargo pod.'

'They're stupid names, don't you think?'

'What are?' she asked, unsure what her companion was talking about.

'You know, Mars' moons, Phobos and Deimos,' he said. 'Why would someone call them that?'

'They're characters in Greek Mythology. The twin sons of Ares. Phobos represents panic and fear, whereas Deimos symbolizes terror and dread.'

'Well, they're aptly named for this place,' he said. 'How do you know this stuff?'

'My dad used to read me stories about Ancient Greece when I was a little girl.'

'Well, they're completely different from the stories my father read to me when I was a kid. I was brought up on tales about war heroes and cowboys. It was his proudest moment when I graduated from the academy.'

'I'm sure he'd be proud of you today.'

There was no reply. She looked across, but he was already asleep.

9.

Bored, Kelly wrote her name with her finger in the moisture which had collected around the edges of the windscreen. Next to her, Mac produced heavy-breathed snores and had done for several hours, his tall frame cramped behind the wheel of the Rover. Unfortunately, for her, sleep had not been forthcoming.

The first signs of daylight spilled through the vent high in the cargo pod wall. From the look of it, the sun had risen enough for them to be able to return to the Aeolis.

'Mac, Mac, wake up,' she said, nudging him with her elbow. 'It's time to go.'

He let out a stifled yawn, stirring from his slumber.

The display on the dashboard showed the batteries now contained only seven percent of charge.

'What's the temperature outside?' she asked.

'Ten below,' he replied, looking at the screen through bleary eyes.

'Perfect. We can head back. Let's get to work.'

There was not enough charge left to attempt towing the second trailer, so they drove back empty-handed. The whole second trip to the cargo pods had been a waste of time, and she had put her and Mac's safety at risk. Tired and frustrated, she was annoyed with herself.

After opening the pod door, Mac gently reversed the vehicle onto the planet's surface, pausing for her to climb back in. Being economical with the throttle, they made their way back across the undulating dunes towards the Aeolis.

Once the light above the internal door had turned green, Kelly and Mac wearily removed their helmets, both relieved to be finally back on board.

'Welcome home,' Kenwyn said as they entered the dining room.

'How was your night in the Rover?' Anna asked with a smirk from the other side of the table.

'Uncomfortable,' Kelly replied grumpily.

'Well, you're here now.' the medic said, rising from his seat. 'Sit yourselves down. There's enough breakfast for everyone.'

Mac and Kelly took their seats as Kenwyn placed trays in front of them.

'Thanks for all your work yesterday,' Kelly said between mouthfuls. 'I really appreciate it, especially with Tony's illness.'

'Morning, you dirty stop-outs,' Wai called, entering the room, her damp hair wrapped in a towel.

Kelly looked sheepishly at the others, not sure what to say about their overnight excursion. 'Today, Anna and Wai, I need you to install the heating units so we can move into the dome,' she said, changing the subject. 'Mac, can you offload the fabricators from the Aeolis. We're going to need to build a workshop, and with Tony out of action, you're going to have to pick up some of his tasks.'

'No worries, Boss,' he said, shoveling a forkful of food into his mouth.

'Once the utilities are online, we can start transferring the supplies over to the dome,' Kelly added. 'Then we can truly call it home.'

'How's the patient this morning?' Wai asked, spooning some food onto her tray.

'A little better, I sat with him all night. His fever has settled, and his blood pressure is less labile, so I've begun weaning him off the inotropes.

'That's excellent news,' Kelly said.

'He's not out of the woods yet though,' he cautioned. 'But it's about as much as we can hope for at the moment.'

'When are you going to wake him?' Kelly asked.

'Let's see how he goes over the next twenty-four hours. If his vital signs remain stable, I'll start turning down the sedation.'

'I need to send a progress report to Mission Control, then I can sit with him while you sleep if you'd like.'

'That would be really appreciated,' the medic smiled.

It was a relief to be back aboard the Aeolis, its familiarity comforting. After a brief breakfast, she retired to her cabin, taking a shower and putting on a clean t-shirt and burgundy flight suit before heading to the Medical Bay. Despite washing thoroughly, she felt grimy, never having really felt clean since her first trip outside. Wherever she looked, there was a layer of ultra-fine red dust. The crew had each developed a dry, irritating cough which Mac had christened 'Mars lung.' It's side effects frequently interrupting radio communications.

Kelly blow-dried her hair before tying it back in a simple ponytail. While getting dressed, she pondered how the dust could get so far inside the ship. Understandably, it would be in the Comms Room, as it would blow in every time the airlock was used, but how could it reach her room on the other side of the ship?

The cardiac monitor continued to chirp reassuringly, but Tony remained comatose, the drugs preventing him from regaining consciousness. His color had improved from when she had last seen him - now he looked asleep rather than desperately ill. The smell of cleaning fluid and the artificial lighting reminded Kelly of visiting her elderly aunt in hospital many years ago. She prayed this would have a different outcome.

She examined her finger after running it along the surface of the workstation in the Medical Bay, her actions prompting a smile, realizing she was turning into her mother. The Medical Bay was dust-free. For some reason, the otherwise ubiquitous dust had not penetrated this far into the ship's interior. Why was this the only place on the Aeolis without a fine dusting of red powder?

Her tired eyes settled on the air vent grill on the

wall opposite. The last twenty-four hours had been exhausting. Curiously, the grills in here were a different shape from those elsewhere on the ship. She mulled that fact over in her tired mind. Of course! There was a separate air conditioning system in here. That was why she could not find any dust in the Medical Bay. It had been designed that way to prevent any airborne diseases being circulated, allowing the unit to be isolated if needed. She made a mental note to ask Mac to create a filter to slot into the air con. Unintentionally, she closed her eyes and the sound of the heart monitor quickly drifted further and further away.

'Hey, come on sleepy head,' a voice said, gently rocking her arm.

'What time is it?' she asked sleepily.

'It's nearly noon.'

'Noon?' her eyes snapped open. The smiling face of Kenwyn greeting her. 'I must've fallen asleep. Tony's been no trouble.'

'Great news,' he said with a knowing wink.

'I have to go and help Anna and Wai,' she said, getting up.

'Kelly,' he said, as she brushed past him. 'It's okay to take care of yourself as well as everyone else.'

She smiled politely but said nothing.

Suited up, Kelly trudged along the path which was beginning to develop between the Aeolis and the dome. After navigating the new airlock, she through the door for the first time. From the outside, the structure was complete, but there was still a lot of work needed inside before it would be habitable. The incredibly spacious interior was a stark contrast to the cramped conditions they had tolerated for the past eight months. A single strip of lights ran the length of the ceiling, emitting scarcely enough light to reach to the edges. Crates and packaging littered the floor, and disconnected cables hung loosely from the walls. This was going to be their home, for the foreseeable future at least, and she knew it would be perfect for the six of them until more permanent dwellings could be built.

Kelly removed her helmet then unzipped her exosuit, letting it hang around her hips as had become fashionable among the crew.

'Ladies, this is looking good.'

'Hi Kelly,' Anna said with a smile. 'We love our new home.'

'What's the radiation reading in here?' the commander asked.

'Much lower than I was expecting,' the engineer replied. 'Similar to the background level on Earth.'

'That's good, these panels seem to be doing their job,' Kelly said, unfastening the thyroid shield she disliked so much. 'What needs doing next?'

'I need some help putting up the last of the ventilation conduits,' said Wai. 'I've managed to do most of them, but it would be quicker with two of us.'

'Okay, let's do it'.

Anna ran out more lengths of cable while Wai and Kelly fixed stainless steel tubes to the dome's roof. Next, the three of them set about erecting the frames for the dividing walls, which created the individual rooms within the dome.

'Did you feel that?' asked Kelly, looking around at her colleagues.

'Feel what?' Anna asked.

'The ground seemed to shake.'

'Your body's just getting used to not being weightless, that's all,' Wai suggested.

'You're probably right,' she said, returning her attention to the wall frame.

Working quickly, they slotted the walls into position, so the internal layout was now visible. Anna and Wai held the last hollow frame in place while Kelly crouched down to secure it. Not accustomed to bending after such a long period of inactivity, she rested her hand on the floor to steady herself. The dome began to shake, minimally at first but grew in intensity rapidly. A stack of ceiling tiles toppled over, barely missing Wai, making her yell out.

'It's a tremor,' Kelly shouted. 'Lie down.'

The shaking intensified, accompanied by a guttural roar from deep, beneath them.

The lights flickered before going out completely and some unknown objects clattering to the floor. In the darkness, something heavy toppled onto Anna, causing her to scream. Unable to help, Kelly groped around until she located the engineer's hand, squeezing it reassuringly.

It only lasted for thirty seconds before the light came back on. The interior of the dome had been left in disarray; a giant waste pipe pinned Anna to the floor. Kelly and Wai rushed to lift the heavy, concrete tube off their colleague.

'Are you okay?' Wai asked as she and Kelly helped

Anna to her feet.

'I think so,' she replied. 'Just a bit shocked.'

'Get Kenwyn to make sure,' Kelly ordered.

'I will.'

A voice crackled over the makeshift intercom.

'Did you guys feel the tremor?' it was the familiar sound of the medic. 'Is everyone okay?'

'We're fine, just a few cuts and bruises,' Kelly said, leaving the mic open. 'I'd appreciate it if you gave Anna the once over.'

'Anna? Is everything okay?'

'She had an altercation with a sewerage pipe.'

'I'm fine,' the engineer shouted.

'Come and see me when you get back to the Aeolis.'

'How's the ship?' Kelly asked.

'No alarms are going off, so I think we're okay. On a more positive note, Tony's sedation has been reduced.'

'That's wonderful news,' she said, speaking louder than usual to ensure Kenwyn could hear her. 'I'll be over once we've finished here.'

'Roger that, was anything damaged?'

'No, the dome seems intact, but we're a little shaken if you'll excuse the pun.'

'When am I going to receive an invite to the housewarming party?'

'Not just yet,' Anna called out, rubbing her bruised arm. 'The place is a mess.'

'Can you ask Mac to start removing the wall panels from the Aeolis so we can use them in the dome?' Kelly asked.

'Sure thing.'

After the final wall frame was in position, Anna and Kelly left Wai to reorganize the disruption, while they suited up and walked outside.

'Where's the best place to put the junction box?' asked Kelly, pulling a large equipment trolley behind her.

'How about here?' Anna asked. 'I can deploy the solar farm on this part of the crater. It seems to get most of the sun this morning.'

The two of them struggled to lift a large, metal casing off the trolley before forcing the long spikes on its base into the dusty ground.

'Can you pass me that wrench?' Anna asked, lying on her back with her head inside the box.

Kelly bent down, handing the tool to her colleague.

'Is it just me,' Anna said. 'Or is this totally exciting? I mean, we're the first people to make a successful landing on the planet.'

'I'm finding it quite overwhelming, if I'm honest, somewhere between extreme excitement and abject fear. It fluctuates between the two constantly.'

'You rarely have one without the other,' Anna observed, tightening a bolt.

'I could do with fewer earthquakes.'

'I'm still not sure we should be doing this,' the engineer said, flinching from the pain in her arm as she wriggled out from the box.

'We could leave it until tomorrow if you're not up to it,' Kelly said.

'No, not that, this whole journey.'

'It's a bit late to be getting cold feet, isn't it?'

Anna sat up, reaching for a length of wire, 'Look at

this place. It's beautiful.

Humans haven't got a good track record of looking after our planets. Hundreds of people will come, we'll terraform it, and very soon it'll stop being Mars and become another over-inhabited version of Earth.'

'I guess that's what the Agency want. If you feel like that, why did you come?'

'I hadn't thought about it until I got here. It's just so breath-taking, it seems a shame to spoil it.'

'We have to make sure we keep it special. We're missing Tony's expertise at the moment, but it's good he's beginning to wake up,' she said, trying to change the subject.

'I'm praying he does,' Anna said, feeding the cables into   the   back   of   the   housing.

10.

Over the next few days, the team spent time furnishing the dome, making it habitable and organized. The lighting, air conditioning and many other utilities were now up and running, reducing their dependency on the Aeolis. Mac had stripped almost all of the wall panels from the spacecraft, leaving wires and pipes exposed in many of the corridors of the ship, and had begun installing them in their new dwelling. Conversely, the interior of the dome was almost finished. It now housed a functioning laboratory to aid scientific research, and the Infirmary had been fully equipped.

Kelly sat in the Comms Room aboard the Aeolis, admiring the sunrise through the airlock. To her surprise, Mac, the kind of person who usually needed to be crowbarred out of bed, was the first of the crew to wake.

'Good morning,' he said, pouring a mug of coffee.

'Morning. Will you look at that view?' she said, staring out of the airlock door.

'It's captivating, isn't it? Much more than I'd ever expected.'

'I know, so different to back home. I find it hard not to stare.'

Mac opened the internal airlock door and stood nearer the outer window.

'We're down to a quarter of our water reserves on the Aeolis, Kelly said without leaving her desk. 'I'm going to need you to find water for us in the next few days.'

'Of course,' he said, finishing what was left in his cup. 'I wasn't being awkward, but we only have the geologists' opinion, and even then, they could only say water was quite likely.'

'If there isn't water, we're all going home, and this whole mission would have been a failure,' Kelly replied flatly. 'Our supplies are such, we'll have to introduce water rationing soon so we can survive until the Discovery arrive.'

'No pressure then,' he said with his usual schoolboy smirk.

Mac sat in front of the computer in the control room of the cargo bay, wearing his now familiar burgundy t-shirt, white knee-length shorts and flip flops. Beside him, another mug of coffee rested on the desktop. He studied the images from the year-old satellite survey, comparing them with the more recent photographs he had taken with his drones, quickly identifying the area where the geologists had suggested there could be water. Thankfully, they did not have to travel far. The region had been named 'El Dorado' by the cartographers in the 1960s due to the yellow sedimentary rock which littered the surface, but it was water, not gold, he hoped to find.

Tapping through some menus, he extended one of Aeolis' external, motorized arms which he had used to unload the contents of the hold. Double-clicking the red icon on the screen, he detached the arm from the craft, causing it to clatter to the ground outside. He and Kelly suited up before securing the hollow, metal cylinder to the back of the Rover.

The arm ploughed a furrow into the subsoil as the vehicle hesitantly descended to a depression on the crater floor. The vehicle plodded across the undulating surface until a red light began to flash on the console, indicating they had arrived at the coordinates identified by the geologists.

'We're here,' Mac said. 'I hope those boffins back on Earth are right.'

'There's only one way to find out,' Kelly commented, slipping her helmet back on.

The two of them unhitched the metal arm then left it lying on the ground amongst the rocks, before jumping back into the vehicle and heading for the cargo site where they had spent the night a few days earlier. At the back of pod number three, they located a peculiar-looking trailer. They heaved it down the ramp, fastened it to the Rover's tow bar then began retracing their tracks to where the arm lay.

'Right, I'll find us some help.' Kelly' said, returning to the Rover, leaving Mac alone on the surface.

Opening the top of the trailer, he locked each half of the lid into position to create the pyramidal drilling rig which stood as tall as a man. After clambering onto the edge of the machine's frame, he extended the telescopic, steel insert which would lock the arm in place.

'Mac,' Kelly said, her voice appearing in his headset.

'What?'

'If you're going to carrying on singing while you work, can you turn your mic off?' she sniggered. 'The rest of us don't need to be subjected to that.'

'How rude?' he replied with mock offence. 'Mac out.'

He pulled out the two halves of the thick, sliding base which acted as supports to prevent the whole assembly from moving while it operated. All that was needed for the rig to be assembled was for the hollow, robotic arm to be inserted into the top. Unable to proceed any further without assistance, he sat on a rocky outcrop, admiring the view.

Long before he could see the Rover, Kelly's return was heralded by an approaching dust cloud. She had recruited Kenwyn and Anna to help with assembling the equipment.

'Okay, let's get to work,' Mac said through his helmet's intercom.

'Of course, but please don't sing,' Kenwyn laughed.

'Man, you guys are brutal,' Mac said.

They fastened chains around the heavy, metal arm on the floor, connecting it to the winch on top of the Rover's cab.

'Careful,' he said to Anna. 'The cutting teeth are on that end, and they're very sharp.'

'We've not done this before with only four of us,' Anna said, readjusting her grip. 'I'm not sure we're strong enough to lift it.'

'Wai has to stay with Tony,' Kelly interjected. 'So,

we have to play the hand we've been dealt.'

Mac opened a panel on the side of the Rover and flicked a switch, bringing the winch to life. One end of the robotic arm lifted slowly off the crater floor while they struggled to maneuver the other end into the hole on the top of the trailer.

They fought with the unwieldy metal tube for over an hour without success before an all too familiar beeping noise began.

'Mac, that's your radiation alarm,' Kelly said. 'You need to take some time out.'

'But we've almost got this. I'll be okay.'

'No, you won't,' she said authoritatively. 'Go and sit in the Rover. That's an order.'

He trudged reluctantly to the protective sanctuary of the vehicle.

'I have an idea,' Kenwyn spoke through heavy breaths.

'What?' Kelly asked, a little too tersely.

'Would you two be able to hold up the arm if I help you lift it?'

'I guess so.'

'Not for too long, though,' said Anna. 'It's extremely heavy.'

The three of them struggled to elevate the end of the metal arm.

'Okay,' Kenwyn said. 'Take the weight.'

Letting go, the medic set about rocking the trailer, heaving it back and forth until it rolled onto its side, then the three of them attempted to slide the metal arm inside the machine.

'I'm going to drop it,' Anna called, shaking with the exertion.

'Just a few more seconds,' he begged.

With one end supported by the Rover's winch, they forced the free end of the arm into the slot on the capsized trailer, locking it into position with a satisfying clunk.

'Well done, everyone. Now we can use the Rover to lift the drilling rig upright,' he explained.

'Excellent,' Kelly said, letting go of the weight.

Exhausted, the three of them rested against the Rover, catching their breath and easing their aching muscles. The rig lay at an awkward angle, the narrow part of the arm still held aloft by the winch, while the broader end with its cutting teeth was secured inside the trailer.

'Impressive work,' Mac's voice crackled across the intercom. 'I felt guilty sitting in here watching.'

'You shouldn't feel guilty. It was punishment for singing into an open mic,' Kenwyn said with a smile.

'Damn,' Mac laughed.

Once rested, Anna used the winch to lift the machine into an upright position, jolting it onto its wheels. The whole assembly now looked like a sailing yacht with a long mast on a sea of red sand.

'Well done, everyone,' Kelly said with her usual chirpiness.

'Anna, I'll drive the boss and Kenwyn back to the Aeolis then I'll come back,' Mac said into the intercom. 'My radiation timeout will be over by the time I return.'

'Okay,' she said, giving him a thumbs-up through the windscreen.

'We can see if there's water on this planet.'

'There better be,' said Kelly bluntly. 'Otherwise, we'll be heading home when the Discovery gets here. That'll be the end of our dream of a colony on Mars.'

'I'm confident,' said Mac.

'You're always confident,' Kenwyn butted in. 'But it's about time those experts back on Earth actually got something right.'

The medic and Kelly joined Mac onboard the Rover, leaving Anna alone on the surface with the drilling rig. Having never been this far from the dome on her own before made her a little anxious. She nervously surveyed her surroundings. Ahead, a dune sloped across the skyline. The ground was much darker there, almost black with faint yellow striations running through it. If this was El Dorado, she hoped it was not fool's gold. It already seemed quite tarnished. Suddenly, the hairs on the back of her neck stood up, as if something terrible was going to happen. She thought she saw something move up ahead, but after staring for a while, realized it was just her mind playing tricks.

It was about forty minutes before Mac parked up next to her.

'What kept you?' she asked.

'I popped in to see Tony. He seems to be doing fine. Kenwyn thinks he's over the worst.'

'That's excellent news,' she replied, still slightly unsettled. 'We'd better get cracking. Otherwise, my radiation alarm is going to go off. We don't want a two-hour cool down before we can start.'

After reconnecting the drilling rig to the Rover's winch, Mac selected the program from a list on the onboard computer. Anna relaxed into the passenger seat, watching as the teeth on the broader end of the arm oscillated back for, cutting into the rocky ground underneath the trailer.

'Make yourself comfortable,' Mac said, climbing inside Rover. Anna's radiation alarm ringing in his ears. 'This could take some time.'

They watched as, inch by inch, the metal was forced underground.

After a long pause, Anna spoke,' What made you want to do this?'

'There's is nothing else I've ever wanted to do. I can't remember considering anything else. When I was a kid, I would sit for hours looking up at the stars wondering what's out there. When I was eight, when most kids were getting footballs, I got a telescope. How about you?'

'I kind of fell into it. Loving physics, I'm fascinated by how things work, so I was happiest as a quantum physicist.'

'Don't you find all that thinking boring? Surely you want to do something other than think?'

'Thought experiments are amazing. Once I was considering string theory when I looked at the clock and realized six hours had passed. I had forgotten to eat, forgotten to drink. It was as if I'd been in a trance. I love the simplicity of the mathematics. It's so pure, almost beautiful.'

'But boring,' Mac said wryly. 'That's not my cup of tea at all. If you love the science so much, how did you end up here?'

'I was the chief physicist at a nuclear power plant in the Samara Region in Russia when some guys from the Agency invited me for an interview. They asked me if I would like to be in charge of the reactor on this mission, and it seemed like a good idea.'

'Wow!' Mac said with fake amusement. 'A good

idea? This has been my dream since childhood, and you make it sound like you were deciding whether to go to the cinema.'

'Sorry, I didn't mean to insult you. That wasn't my intention. Our lives have been different, that's all. For you, this was a life goal, whereas, for me, I drifted into it. Honestly, I'm glad to be here.'

He looked suspiciously at her.

'No, I really am! For me, it's more about the people than it is about the task,' Anna said, taking two energy bars out of the arm pockets of her exosuit.

'Are you saying you came to Mars to make friends,' Mac asked.

'No,' she smiled, offering one to him. 'But when you work in such a male-orientated field as nuclear physics you have to do what you can to have a diverse group of friends.'

'How do you mean?'

'Well, otherwise I'd be surrounded by physicists all my life.'

'Too nerdy?'

'No, I quite like nerds, but they tend to be devoid of fashion sense. You know, all jackets with elbow pads and brown shoes.'

'That's not a good look,' he smiled. 'Anyway, the nuclear reactor will be heading back to Earth when the Aeolis leaves in a couple of weeks. That should reduce your workload.'

'We have to set up the solar farms first. Our next biggest deadline.'

'I don't know why the Agency doesn't let us use the reactor here permanently.'

'They want to keep Mars as clean as possible. Something I agree with. We've ruined one planet; we can't destroy another.'

'I'll be sad to see the Aeolis go. I've come to think of her as home.'

'It's all about the costs. If the ships are reusable, then the cost of flying to here is considerably less.'

'I know, but the ship has been our home for so long, and we've been through so much together.'

'You're too sentimental. This is our home now.'

When the red light on her radiation timer finally stopped blinking, there was still no evidence of water. With no reason to venture back outside, they sat comfortably in the silence, watching the metal arm as it painstakingly worked its way into the ground.

***

'How are you feeling?' Kenwyn asked, standing alongside the bed.

'Much better,' Tony replied groggily.

'Well, your vital signs have returned to normal, and your pain seems reasonably well-controlled, so I want you to try standing.'

'Are you sure?'

'Absolutely,' he said, flashing a reassuring smile.

Arms open wide, the medic was ready to catch his superior officer if he should stumble. Tony struggled to the edge of the bed, grimacing as he rested both feet on the cold, metal floor. Planting his feet on the steel plate, he pushed down into his legs. He grimaced and grunted before slumping back onto the bed.

'Don't worry, that's to be expected. Take your time.'

After catching his breath, he tried again, bearing down, forcing himself onto his feet with a defiant shout.

'How do you feel now you're upright?'

'Good, but it hurts like hell,' Tony said, sweating profusely.

'Any light-headedness or dizziness?'

'Nope, only pain in my belly.'

'A lot?'

'No, only when my heart beats,' he attempted to laugh, but the pain stopped him abruptly.

'Don't worry, I'll increase your medication.'

11.

'I have a bad feeling about this,' Anna said reluctantly.

'Yep. If there was water here, we would've hit it by now,' replied Mac.

Disappointed, they watched the final meter of metal slowly disappear into the dirt.

'Do you think we will finish everything before the Aeolis heads back?' she asked. 'Tony's illness is going to delay everything; we won't be able to start building the residential block for a few weeks.'

'That wouldn't be the end of the world. The colonists can live on the Discovery until things are ready.'

'I'm more worried about whether we've got enough water to last until they arrive, there's nothing here.'

Mac erupted into a bout of coughing.

'This dust is annoying,' he said, clearing his throat.

'Oh! It really is. My hair always feels gritty, even when I haven't been outside.'

'It gets everywhere, doesn't it?'

Suddenly, a fountain of fluid erupted from the top of the drilling rig, cascading onto the barren, red surface.

'Look at that!' Mac exclaimed, slamming his hand down on the Rover's console.

'Excellent,' she said, giving him a tight embrace.

Mac slipped on his helmet and exited through the rear of the vehicle before capping off the jet of water gushing from the head of the drilling rig.

'Well done,' Anna said as he climbed back into the driver's seat. 'You'd better let the others know.'

'Kelly?' he spoke into the intercom. 'Are you there?'

'Where else would I be? What's up?'

'The boffins back on Earth were right,' Mac said calmly. 'We have water!'

'Hey, everyone, they've successfully tapped the aquifer,' she said excitedly to those around her, their cheers distorting the speakers.

'That's fantastic news. When the Discovery arrives, it will be to expand the colony, not take us home.'

'I think we should throw a party tonight to celebrate,' Anna suggested. 'Especially now Tony's getting better.'

'Great idea,' Kelly said.

'Let's hold it in the Medical Bay, then Tony can attend,' Wai said in the background.

'Well done, Mac!' Kenwyn's voice appeared. 'But I think it'll be too much for him. He'll become exhausted very quickly. So, let's celebrate in the Comms Room, then Tony will be able to leave when he gets tired.'

'Perfect,' said Kelly.

'Mac,' Kenwyn continued. 'Bring me some samples. I'll need to analyze them.'

'Will do.'

***

Wearing a full Hazchem suit, Kenwyn stared at the six flasks of sludgy-brown water resting on the worktop in the Aeolis' small diagnostic area.

'I wonder what mysteries you hold,' he muttered to himself. He pipetted liquid from each one into individual vials. After centrifuging them, he placed the tubes inside the biochemical analyzer on the counter. Next, using some of the remaining water, he made a microscope slide.

Turning a flywheel, he brought the film into focus. The field displayed on the screen in front of him contained a few tiny pieces of rock debris, but nothing else of note. He changed slides, mumbling to himself as he captured his notes on the computer.

'Don't be too long,' Mac called from the doorway. 'There's some serious celebrating to do.'

'You're not meant to be in here,' Kenwyn replied sternly, his voice muffled inside the suit's hood. 'We don't know whether it's biologically safe.'

'Loosen up. Are you coming to the party?'

'I'll be there as soon as I'm done here,' the medic said. 'Now clear off.'

'Can I take Tony with me?'

'Yes, use the collapsible wheelchair, but keep an

eye on him. The first sign of him getting tired and I want him straight back here, okay?'

'Will do,' Mac chuckled, disappearing out of the door. 'Don't work too hard.'

The lighting had been turned down low and someone had draped a string of lights around the large screen behind Kelly's desk. Everyone knew unnecessary equipment had not been allowed on board the Aeolis, but this addition certainly made it feel more relaxed.

'You can't have a party without us,' Mac announced, wheeling Tony into the dimly-lit room.

The three women cheered as Mac positioned the wheelchair next to them, struggling to find the break with his foot.

'How are you?' Wai asked, putting her arm around Tony's shoulder.

'Not too bad. I just get tired easily.'

'Do you want a beer?'

'It's probably not a good idea with all the painkillers I'm on. Maybe some water.'

'I don't mind if I have one though,' Mac said cheekily, grabbing a bottle from the table.

'Help yourself,' Kelly said before devouring some popcorn.

'Where's Kenwyn?'

'He's running some tests on those water samples. He shouldn't be long.'

Music blared from the ship's tinny intercom when the medic finally arrived at the party. The desks had been pushed to the side of the room, creating space for Mac, Anna and Wai to dance. Kelly knelt beside the wheelchair, deep in conversation with Tony. A further cheer erupted when Kenwyn entered the room, the alcohol loosening the group's usual inhibitions. Popping a handful of peanuts into his mouth, he joined his colleagues on the dance floor.

A new track began to play. Kenwyn and Anna smiled at each other across the room. They took to the center of the makeshift dancefloor while the others stood back. The two of them were well-known within the Agency for their dance routines. Their sequence at the previous Christmas celebrations had been particularly memorable, spawning rumors that their relationship was more than friendship. They danced together, improvising a routine, their eyes wide, never leaving each other. The rest of the crew clapped along from the edge, drinks in hand. When the music stopped, they ended in a prolonged clinch, prompting a cheer to erupt around them. Kenwyn bowed, obviously breathing hard and Anna performed an elaborate curtsey.

'It's wonderful to see you out of the Medical Bay,' Kelly shouted over the din, leaning in towards the assistant commander. 'I'm glad you're on the mend. You gave us quite a scare.'

Tony smiled, the loud music making it difficult for him to be heard.

'How are you holding up?' the medic shouted over the noise, still breathless.

'Okay, but I'm feeling a bit washed out.'

'I'll take you back in a couple of minutes. First, I need a few words with Kelly.'

'Excuse me for a moment,' she apologized before

following after him.

They leant against the bulkhead on opposite sides of the narrow corridor, facing each other. Kelly closed the door, blocking out most of the noise.

'What's up?'

'I've run some preliminary tests on the water Mac brought back. Firstly, there is no bacterial life, so we haven't found life on Mars.'

'I'm not sure whether I'm happy or disappointed by that.'

'The mineral content is tolerable. It might cause a stomach upset for a few days, but we'll soon become used to it.'

'Okay,' she said. 'Why do I feel I'm waiting for a 'but?''

'It has a higher radiation reading than I would expect from the type of rock we found it in.'

'How high?'

'Our filters will remove it, so it is drinkable, but it's a concern, don't you think?'

'That's odd. The surface levels are well within the limits we expected,' Kelly said, pausing as she mulled it over. 'Do you think the Aeolis could be the source?'

'I don't think so, the surface levels would be up if we were the cause. So, that would suggest it's coming from underground.

Kelly pondered silently then said, 'Can we keep this to ourselves? We don't want to worry the rest of the crew unnecessarily. I'll discuss it with the Agency and see what they suggest.'

12.

'Before you go, can I talk to you about something?' Kelly said, putting down her spoon.

'Sure,' Anna replied, resting back in her seat at the dinner table.

'The water Mac brought back has a higher level of radiation than we're expecting, around ten thousand picocuries per liter.'

'Interesting. In the grand scheme of things, it's a relatively low amount,' she said, her Slavic accent thick and labored. 'But more than you should drink on a regular basis, mind you.'

'Could it be from our reactor? Perhaps we've vented some radioactivity or something,' Kelly's superficial knowledge of the workings of the reactor were becoming evident.

'Unlikely, but I can check again. We've had nothing to suggest there's been a leak. If we did, alarms would be going off.'

'Can you make sure?'

'Of course. It is much more likely to be coming

from an exogenous source.'

'How do you mean?'

'The surface levels are normal, so the cause must be underground.'

'That's what Kenwyn thought. Any ideas what it could be?'

'It could be one of a thousand things.'

Wai wandered amongst shelving units festooned with plant pots in the newly erected greenhouse. The long, plexiglass hall extended for a hundred meters, adjacent to the back of the dome, with additional storage rooms next to the connecting door. Having sown seeds for weeks before they landed, cereal, fruit and vegetable seedlings were beginning to poke through the soil. She allowed herself to be excited, this was the opportunity of a lifetime, not to mention the immense joy the lack of weeds brought.

These were precious. These were the beginnings of sustainable agriculture on Mars. Her team had spent many years cultivating different species and storing seeds capable of tolerating high levels of radiation. This crop had a germination rate of eighty-three percent, even higher than she had dreamt. These hybrids and their subsequent generations would allow food production even before the planet was fully terraformed.

'Wai, are you in here?' Kelly called with a friendly tone.

'Yes, over here,' she said, placing the spray mister on the shelf in front of her.

Kelly admired the fledgling plants as she sauntered through the greenhouse, 'These are looking excellent, aren't they?'

'It's early days, but so far so good,' the botanist said with her usual coolness.

'I've just finished talking to Kenwyn. He says you'll be able to connect your sprinkler system up later today. He and Mac are connecting the pipe from the aquifer to the dome. Then we'll have running water.'

'Fantastic.'

'There is a small problem though. The water has a slightly higher level of radioactivity than we were expecting.'

'Is it dangerous?'

'Only if we drink large amounts straight from the head of the drilling rig. Kenwyn's connected a series of filters to our water management system. They turn the mildly radioactive brown sludge which comes out of the ground into crystal clear, drinking water.'

'And you're certain it's safe?'

'He and Anna both assure me it's fine.'

'Good. How much water is there underground?

'The Agency's geologists say there's enough to support a whole city for decades. That gives us loads of time to terraform the planet, and when that happens, we'll have rain which should refill the aquifer.'

'But that's at least a decade away.'

'Of course. But right now, you don't need to worry. With the waste recycling system and the reserves Mac has found, we'll have plenty of water for many years to come.'

'Does having a sustainable water supply mean we'll be returning the Aeolis soon?'

'Yes, I think we're ready. To be honest, there's not much left onboard.'

'I'm worried about sending the ship back. It's our safety net if things go wrong.'

'I know, but this has always been the deal. If we hadn't found water, we couldn't have flown back in the Aeolis anyway. There wouldn't have been enough for the journey home. We would still have had to wait for the Discovery.'

'Sending us with only enough water for a one-way trip has always bothered me.'

'That's why the colonists are only a few weeks behind us. I don't want to contradict the chairman, but we're the vanguard, not pioneers.'

'Vanguard,' Wai repeated, considering the word and all its connotations. 'I like it, but losing the Aeolis will be like cutting the umbilical cord.'

'You sure everything's okay? You don't usually worry.'

'I'm missing home,' she responded after a long pause. 'I can't put my finger on what, but Mars is just so.....so alien.'

'I know what you mean. We've all found it difficult, you know, adapting to our new environment, but as more systems come online, then the more it'll feel like home. Soon, the Discovery will be here, and then we'll be looking at colony expansion. When that happens, I'm really going to need you.'

'Thanks,' Wai said, blinking back the tears. 'Don't you ever get a little weepy?'

Kelly gave her a hug, Wai reciprocating much more forcibly than the commander expected.

'Of course I do, but you can always talk to me. We'll only survive this if we're open and honest with each other.'

'Thanks,' she said, embracing her again.

Slipping on her exosuit, Kelly proceeded through the dome's airlock. Outside, the Rover drove slowly, pulling what looked like a plough behind it, cutting a dark red line in the ground.

'Mac, how's it going?' she asked over the intercom.

'I've nearly finished digging the trench for the water pipe. We should have this completed today.'

'Great.'

'Once we've buried it, the water won't freeze during the cold nights.'

Kelly turned to walk across to the Aeolis and for a brief second, she thought she saw a hooded figure high up on the ridge of mountains on the crater's edge. She blinked hard, but when she opened her eyes, the person was gone.

'Kenwyn?' she said into her microphone. 'Where are you?'

'I'm in the Medical Bay on the Aeolis with Tony. We're about ready to transfer to the dome.'

'Roger that,'

'Anna? What's your location?'

A channel went quiet for several seconds before Anna's accented English appeared in Kelly's ear, 'Hi, I'm in the Reactor Room. Everything's running smoothly. There is no sign of the radiation coming from here.'

'Thanks.'

'Hallucinations!' Kelly muttered to herself. 'Has it come to this? I must get more sleep.'

13.

The long shadows on the crater floor began to retreat as the sun rose above the Columbia Hills. Anna and Mac had woken early and set off in search of the cause of the high radiation levels in the water.

'The Geiger counter's chirping more than I would expect,' she said. 'But there's nothing obvious causing it.'

'It's like looking for a needle in a haystack,' Mac observed. 'There's got to be something around here causing it.'

The device ticked faster as Mac stumbled across a mound of spoil from the trench he had ploughed the previous day. A thought struck him. It was just a hunch, but they had few other explanations for the phenomenon they were encountering. He jogged back to the Rover, retrieving a spade from inside the vehicle then began digging close to the housing which now covered the water pipe they had sunk the day before. The mixture of sand and small rocks cascaded onto the ground as he sunk the blade into the ground.

'The level's gone up,' Anna said, running the meter a few inches above the disturbed soil. We should get some of this back to the lab so we can have a closer look at it.'

They hurriedly shoveled some of the dirt into a couple of white, sample collection boxes, snapping the lids shut before tucking them inside Mac's rucksack.

Anna bent down, picking up a strange-looking, black rock from the surface, placing it carefully onto the floor of the vehicle.

'Do you think it's the soil?' Mac asked, starting the engine.

'I think so, but I'd like to study it some more.'

'What's your best guess?'

'You'll just have to wait and see,' she said mysteriously.

'You're no fun,' he smiled.

Like the rest of the dome, the walls of the laboratory were clad with the panels stripped from the Aeolis. Mac slumped at a desk and, under the desk-mounted magnifying glass, he studied the large rock. He turned the smooth mineral over in his hand, examining it from all perspectives, looking for clues as to what it was. It had multiple-angular facets, each with a strange, metallic luster set in a yellow, granular matrix. The meter spiked abruptly as he passed the Geiger counter over its surface. Bending down, he slid open a drawer in the workstation and removed a diamond-edged cutting tool. He used the device to excise a fragment of the mineral and then handed it to Anna, who placed it onto the stage of the microscope.

Turning the wheel back and forth, she brought the small piece into focus on the screen on the wall. Its characteristic appearance was immediately recognizable, confirming her suspicions.

'Well, that's the source of the radiation,' she said, pointing at the screen.

'What is it?' Mac asked, leaning over her shoulder.

'Pitchblende. More commonly known as Uranium Oxide.'

'Uranium?' he repeated, his voice faltering. 'Are we safe having it in here?'

'Obviously, you want to minimize the amount of exposure you have, but we're perfectly safe handling a piece this size for a short period. It's only weakly radioactive.'

'So, we're sitting on a huge uranium deposit?'

'Yep, but our shielding is more than enough to protect us. We have nothing to worry about.'

'We should tell Kelly.'

He walked to the other side of the room and held down a button on the intercom, 'Hi Kelly, I need you in the laboratory.'

'Okay, on my way,' her voice appearing over the speaker.

'So, what you're telling me is we have a large deposit of uranium on our doorstep,' the commander said, looking at her two colleagues.

They both nodded.

'And you're sure we're safe?'

'Yes,' Anna said, 'The metal baseplate and the lead lining of the walls will keep out the radiation, and the exosuits are more than capable of keeping out these levels.'

'Well, the Agency will be extremely interested,' Kelly said. 'The value of this deposit alone is likely to cover the cost of this mission. I suspect we'll see opencast mining here very soon.'

'More destruction,' Anna grumbled. 'If we're not careful we're going to trash this planet too. We seem to have learnt nothing from Earth.'

'I thought we came here to find resources like this,' Mac said, puzzled by Anna's reaction.

'I agree,' Kelly added, somewhat puzzled.

'But we're going to scar this place before we even understand it,' Anna said unhappily. 'What if there's life here? We might kill it off before we've had a chance to study it.'

'You've been outside. Did you see any signs of life?' Mac asked; Kelly deliberately keeping out of the discussion. 'The planet's lifeless.'

'Even if there's no surface life, what about in the subsoil or around underground vents? We've no way of knowing. All that would be lost.'

'The presence of life on Mars is a hypothesis,' he tried to explain, trying to appeal to her scientific nature. 'What should we do? Preserve the planet as a museum on the off-chance there being life here?'

'I understand the need for progress. I really do, but what if there's bacteria or algae containing compounds which could cure cancer? We're scientists, and we're meant to research, not destroy.'

Kelly left Anna to simmer for a few hours before seeking her out again. Adjusting to the new life was having its toll on her. Later that afternoon, Kelly found her sitting in the reactor room on the Aeolis.

'How are you doing?' Kelly asked, closing the door

behind her.

'I'm okay. I'm sorry about my outburst earlier.'

'It's alright, you're clearly passionate about safeguarding this planet.'

The engineer remained quiet before asking, 'Have you ever been to Krasnodar in Russia?'

'I can't say I have,' Kelly replied, slightly thrown by the question. 'Tell me about it,'

'It's a huge, industrial port in the south of the country. It sits on the banks of the Kuban river. There's a park on a spit of land which extends out into the water. When I was a kid, my father and I used to sit and watch the container ships transport freight down the river. Sometimes we'd fish, other times we would swim. It was a magical place. Around a decade ago, a tanker ran aground not far from the park, spilling more than a hundred million liters of crude oil into the river. They tried to clean it up, but it got into the soil. It contaminated everything. All the small creatures that no one cares about, the mollusks and worms, were poisoned. The fish which fed on these died, so the birds left. Now the whole area is barren. What had been my special place, where a lot of my childhood memories were made, is now a toxic nightmare of black tar and decay. I don't want the same thing to happen here.'

Kelly nodded, absorbing Anna's story.

'I understand,' she said finally. 'We're here now, and more than a hundred colonists are only a few weeks behind us. So, I guess we have a responsibility to make sure that doesn't happen.'

'What did you have in mind?'

'Once we have power and we send the Aeolis back, I would like you to draw up a charter for how research can be done with the minimum of damage to the planet. There will always be mining, and the long-term plan is to terraform, but I would like you to create the rules of the game.'

'Will the Agency be happy with that?'

'Probably not,' Kelly said honestly. 'But leave them to me.'

'Thanks, Kelly,' she said, giving her a hug.

Walking back through the Aeolis' bare corridors, Kelly bumped into Tony and Kenwyn.

'Where are you two gentlemen heading?'

'Tony's officially discharged from the Medical Bay,' the medic said. 'So, he's going over to the dome for the first time.'

'Great, I'll walk with you,' she said. 'Tony, how are you feeling?'

'I'm okay, just a little bit sore.'

'It's good to see you back on your feet. You gave us all quite a scare.'

The three of them put on their exosuits, the assistant commander struggling a little before Kenwyn decompressed the airlock.

'Do you recall being down on the surface?' Kelly asked.

'Not at all,' Tony replied. 'I can't even remember the landing.'

'Well, you helped build this dome,' she said. 'You collapsed as we were putting the last panel into place.'

'This place looks fantastic,' he said, not remembering the landscape.

'The appearance changes throughout the day,' Kenwyn said. 'There's something about the evening sunlight which brings the place alive.'

They followed the floor lights, moving slower than usual to accommodate for Tony's lack of pace.

'I'll catch you guys later,' said Kelly when they arrived, shedding her exosuit before walking into the narrow corridor. She crossed the empty dining room, through the metal door into the residential block. The late afternoon sun shone through the plexiglass ceiling, providing welcome relief from the otherwise artificial light inside the dome. Exhausted, she fell onto her bed. It seemed that most of her time that day had been spent acting as a therapist to the other members of the crew. She had never been trained to deal with this.

That evening, the entire crew had dinner together for the first time in their new home. The had arranged the tables into a circle.

'What a momentous few day,' she said. 'We now have running water, and all our power comes from solar panels.'

'Yep,' said Anna. 'The dome's batteries are fully charged, and in the morning, I'll disconnect the reactor.'

'Well done, everyone,' Kelly said, rising from her seat. 'I propose a toast.'

They all stood, apart from Tony.

'We've had some major successes already. Creating power independently and having a native supply of water are two key milestones in the establishment of the first sustainable settlement on Mars. Despite a few setbacks, we're still ahead of schedule, and our achievements vastly outnumber our failures. I'm very proud of each and every one of you. To Mars!"

14.

Taking a brief period of respite, Kelly curled up in her quarters, reading a book on waste management. Downtime had become a rare luxury since they had landed, and she relished the opportunity to relax.

'Commander to the Ops Room, immediately,' a female voice crackled over the dome's speaker system.

On hearing the tone of whoever made the announcement, she sprung to her feet and hurried down the corridor.

'What?' she panted, entering the room.

'All the Geiger counters on the surface have maxed out,' Anna said anxiously. 'I can't make sense of it.'

'What are the levels inside the dome.'

'Everything's normal in here. But outside, the readings are sky-high.'

'Could it be a solar flare?'

'Maybe, but the pattern's different from anything I've seen before.'

'Okay, we're safe in here. Is anyone out there at the

moment?'

'Mac's up at the cargo site. He's testing his drones. I think he's planning on surveying the other side of the planet.'

She reached for the intercom, 'Mac, it's Kelly. Can you give me a status report?'

'Hi Kelly,' he replied. 'All's good.'

'We're seeing ridiculous levels of surface radiation. Get in the Rover and come back here ASAP.'

'Sorry, Kelly. Your signal broke up,' Mac's voice crackled with static. 'You're seeing ridiculous levels of what?'

'Radiation!' she shouted. 'Get yourself back here now.'

A garbled message came back amongst a lot of static.

'Mac, come in?' she pleaded. 'Mac?'

Nothing.

'Kelly, you have to come and see this,' Tony said sternly from the doorway, his face white and drained.

'What is it?'

'I have no idea.'

She followed him to the airlock where Kenwyn was staring out through the plexiglass, disbelief etched on his face.

'Oh, My God!' she shrieked. 'Look at it!'.

Through the giant window, a vast storm front advanced rapidly towards their position, the likes of which she had never encountered. Sixty-mile an hour winds propagated a dust cloud several storeys high towards the dome, obscuring the sunlight and concealing the horizon. Lightning forked periodically inside the swirling maelstrom, transiently illuminating the tempestuous landscape.

'He's out in this,' Tony said. 'We have to warn him.'

'I can't reach him,' stressed Kelly. 'But we need to keep trying.'

'I'm on with it,' Kenwyn said, heading for the Ops Room.

'No one is to leave,' Kelly ordered. 'Is that clear?'

'What about Mac?' said Tony. 'We can't just abandon him.'

'No-one leaves!' she repeated adamantly. 'That's an order. We can't help him while it's like this. He'll have to look after himself. He can use the Rover for shelter, we just have to hope this passes quickly.'

'Hope? All you can suggest is hope?' the assistant commander screamed at her. 'You're condemning him to death.'

'Tony!' Kelly said firmly. 'Remember who you are talking to.'

He shook his head, pushing past her, exiting the room.

'You know it's the right call, Boss,' Anna said sympathetically. 'He's just worried about his friend, that's all.'

'Thanks.'

'I'm afraid I have more bad news,' the engineer said hesitantly. 'The dust storm is so dense the solar panels are only working at twenty percent of maximum.'

'That's all I need,' her voice urgent and focused. 'How much power is stored in the batteries?'

'Thankfully, they're full.'

'Okay, shut down all non-essential systems,' Kelly said. 'Leave the airlock operational in case Mac makes it back, but otherwise, we'll only need safety lighting and breathable air. Drop the heating to five degrees and turn off the climate control and waste recycling.'

'Will do,' the engineer said. 'It's going to be pretty uncomfortable.'

'Yep, cold, dark and smelly.'

***

The first he knew about it was when the radiation sensor on his suit began chirping. Mac turned to find a swirling wall of red dust almost upon him. This must have been what Kelly was trying to warn him about. He knew his only hope was the Rover.

The cloud rapidly surrounded him, the light from his helmet's visor not bright enough to penetrate the darkness. The strong winds peppered him with small stones lifted from the planet's surface. Fighting his way through the storm, he located the vehicle by walking into it, such was his visibility. He felt along the fuselage, finding the handle on the back. He instinctively took a deep breath before entering, heaving the door shut behind him. Relieved, he made his way to the front, sealing himself in the cab before flicking the switch to re-pressurize the interior.

After removing his helmet, Mac attempted to reach the dome using the Rover's radio, hoping its better range would help, but it was futile. Frustrated, he tried to start the engine, but it only coughed before dying. The battery levels seemed okay, so he waited a few moments before pressing the ignition button again. This time it fired to life with a little persuasion from Mac's foot toying with the throttle.

Immersed in the dense, swirling cloud, he could see none of the familiar landmarks through the windshield. Nonetheless, he set off, turning one-hundred and eighty degrees before moving slowly towards where he anticipated the Aeolis to be, the Navigation Computer useless.

After an hour, Mac realized he was lost. The storm still shrouded the landscape, blinding and disorientating him. He could be right next to the dome and be unable to tell. The radio remained useless, only harsh static audible over the dashboard speakers. Thankfully, there was enough energy and oxygen aboard the Rover for around eighteen hours, with an additional four left in the cylinder on his exosuit if it came to that. With nothing else to do, he would have to sit it out.

***

Kelly updated the crew, leaning against the edge of her desk in the Ops Room, their faces reflecting the grimness of their current situation.

'Anna, any improvement from the solar panels?' the commander asked.

'Nope, but they're holding at around twenty percent of maximum,' the engineer said. 'Everything's been dialed back to stay within this limit.'

'Thanks. We'd better prepare for it to become mighty cold,' the commander said. 'We've had to turn the water pumps off. So, we can only use bottled water until the storm clears.'

'What? No showers?' Wai exclaimed.

'Nope. We don't have enough power to run them
    and the carbon dioxide scrubbers at the same
time.'

'I guess if we have to choose between breathing
and washing, we'd all elect to breathe,' Tony said
sarcastically, failing to hide his anger.

'Our power levels are critical,' she said, ignoring
him. 'We have barely enough to keep us alive until it
passes. There can be no non-essential usage. Is that
clear?'

Everyone agreed.

'We still have no broadcast function,' Kenwyn said.
'The atmospheric conditions are preventing us from
transmitting.'

So, we are completely isolated here,' Kelly added. 'I
can't even let the Agency know.'

'Their satellites will have picked up the storm,'
Anna commented.

'Any news on Mac?' Wai asked.

'Nope, the last we heard from him was several
hours ago when the storm hit,' Kelly said glumly.
'We've had no contact since.'

'We should be out there looking for him,' the
assistant commander said abruptly.

'Tony, I hear what you're saying,' the medic
interrupted. 'But we'd be putting the rest of us at risk.
Mac has the Rover, and he's up by the cargo pods.
Hopefully, he can find some shelter and sit out the
storm.'

'You're wrong. He's in danger, and we're doing
nothing.'

'Tony, there's nothing we can do,' Wai said, trying
to help her colleague see reason. 'We'd be dead within
minutes of stepping outside.'

'I can't believe you don't care. You're condemning him to death.'

'What do you think we should do?' Kelly asked, struggling to stay composed. 'We're all concerned about him, but we can't risk sending anyone out there.'

Tony stormed out of the room, leaving them behind.

'I don't know what to do with him,' she said desperately.

'He's only worried about Mac,' Kenwyn said. 'Once he's calm down, then he'll realize this is the only thing we can do. I'll talk to him later.'

After an awkward pause, Kelly spoke, 'We have to carry on. We have no additional energy for warming water or cooking. So, until this passes, our food options are going to be a little bleak.'

'Sounds like you're saying we're back on cold rations,' Wai commented.

'Unfortunately, that's exactly what I'm saying. We really are in survival mode until the storm blows over.'

Kenwyn found him standing in the cold airlock, peering out into the swirling, brown dust.

'Any sign of him?' the medic asked, his footsteps on the metal floor sounding hollow.

'Nothing,' Tony said. 'I'm hoping the Rover's lights will appear any moment.'

They stood in silence, their noses against the window.

'You know the way you spoke to Kelly earlier was out of order,' he said, choosing his words carefully.

'Yeah, but we can't leave Mac out there.'

'What else can we do? Going out in this would be suicidal. Mac's smart enough, he'll be okay, I bet he's sitting out the storm in the Rover as we speak.'

'I hope so. I surely hope so.'

15.

The wind howled outside, throwing small rocks against the outer skin of the dome, creating a sound reminiscent of hailstones falling on a tin roof. Each of the crew had retired to their rooms, the lack of heat and power making it almost impossible to work. Kelly had given up trying to send a message to the Agency, the absent signal becoming increasingly frustrating., Despite being fully dressed, she snuggled under the bedclothes, sheltering from the cold.

There was a firm knock at the door, disturbing her thoughts, 'Come in,' she called, sitting up.

Anna entered, clearly anxious about something, closing the door behind her.

'Boss, I'm glad you're in here,' the blonde engineer said, speaking in barely more than a whisper. 'I didn't want to scare the others.'

'What's up?' Kelly asked, seeing the concern on the young woman's face.

'We have a serious problem,' she said, her voice wavering. 'The storm is affecting the reactor on the

Aeolis.'

'How exactly?' the commander said, leaving her bed.

'The reactor's core temperature is rocketing.'

'Why don't you lower some more control rods?' Kelly said, remembering her training.

'For some reason I can't fathom, they won't insert, so it keeps getting hotter. I've been tracking it for the last few hours, and it's not slowing.'

'What are you saying?'

'If I can't, the extra heat will cause the pressure inside the reactor to rise. To cut a long story short, if things don't change, we could have a catastrophe.'

'A meltdown?'

'Yes, but it gets worse,' Anna said.

'I don't think I want to hear this.'

'The coolant turbine which keeps the reactor's temperature down is also not working.'

'So, you're telling me there are two issues,' Kelly summarized succinctly. 'We can't control the rate of reaction, and the cooling system is broken.'

'Absolutely.'

'Any idea why this is happening?'

'It's puzzling me, but they do share some common wiring, so the only thing I can think of is a lightning strike may have hit the Aeolis and fried the circuitry.'

'I thought they were designed to withstand that kind of thing.'

'Me too. It must have been a lucky shot.'

'All right, let's focus. How long do we have before this turns apocalyptic?'

'If the temperature continues to rise at this rate, the reactor vessel is likely to fracture in around two hours.'

'Two hours?'

'Probably less.'

'Hell. What do we need to do?'

'Most functions can normally be carried out from here in the dome, but nothing's working.'

'What about the protocol for emergency shut down?' Kelly asked.

'The SCRAM protocol? I've tried. That relies on the elevators to raise and lower the control rods into the reactor. But there's no power going to them, so the SCRAM button isn't doing anything.'

'How about venting some of the steam to reduce the pressure inside the reactor?'

'Again, it all runs off the same circuit. The elevators, the SCRAM switch, the coolant turbines and the motorized release valve are all dead. I need to go over there and see if I can lower them manually.'

'You want to go outside in the middle of this storm?'

'If I don't, it will be catastrophic, and Mars wouldn't be colonizable for the next hundred thousand years.'

'I understand,' Kelly said, leaning forward. She pressed the intercom button. 'Can all crew report to the Ops Room ASAP, please?'

One by one, they arrived; some wore blankets over their shoulders, others dressed in hats and gloves to keep warm, their breath visible in the cold air. Tony, the last to appear, winced from the exertion of hurrying along the corridor.

'I was hoping you were going to say Mac was here,' he said disappointedly.

'Sadly not, but we have another urgent situation,' said Kelly. 'Anna must go over to the Aeolis to fix the reactor. If she doesn't, there is a significant risk of a meltdown. It would be better if someone went with her.'

'I'll go,' Tony said, without hesitating.

'I don't think you're well enough,' Kenwyn interrupted. 'I'll go.'

The assistant commander went to protest but quickly decided against it.

'Okay,' Kelly said, looking around the room. 'That's decided then.'

16.

Anna, Kenwyn and Kelly slipped on their exosuits quickly followed by their helmets. Tony and Wai wished them luck before retreating to the safety of the corridor. Kelly fastened retractable ropes, no thicker than washing lines, to the loops on the back of the other two's suits - a precaution, in case one of them became lost in the storm.

'If our communication with Mac is anything to go by, our intercoms won't work out there,' Kelly said, using the microphone in her helmet. 'We'll be unable to talk to each other, so three sharp tugs mean you've run into difficulty. Five tells me you've made it, okay?'

They both agreed.

'Don't set off until I've secured you to the outside of the dome,' she added. 'I can't afford to lose any more crew members in this storm.'

They nodded again.

'Good luck,' Kelly said, pulling down the lever.

She watched apprehensively as her two crewmates disappeared into the tempest. Instantly, the swirling cloud flooded over them, forcing them to bend at the waist as they steadied themselves against the wind. She secured the free ends of the two tethers to hooks on the dome's external wall, normally used for holding shutters in place. She tried the intercom just on the off chance it would work, but only received static. Now they were on their own.

Holding hands, Anna and Kenwyn moved incredibly slowly, edging forward one step at a time, their visibility virtually zero. To make matters worse, they were continually bombarded with debris thrown up by the winds. The ground lights provided little more than an indistinct glow at their feet, but enough to reassure them they were heading in the right direction across the constantly changing landscape. Kelly gripped a rope in each hand, Anna's in her left hand and Kenwyn's in her right. Reassuringly, she could feel the cord running freely through her gloved fingers.

Every so often, lightning would strike around them, illuminating the grotesque, eddying dust storm. They were approximately halfway when Anna's hand slipped out of Kenwyn's grip. He instinctively reached out but grasped fruitlessly at the dense air. Constantly buffeted by the high winds, he crouched awkwardly, desperately searching for her.

The rope in Kelly's left hand went slack, followed shortly by the tension leaving the other too. Not enough had passed through her fingers for them to have reached the Aeolis. Fear rose inside her, as both ropes had lost their tautness for far too long. She did not know what to do, should she attempt to find them?

Kenwyn's gloves sank into the dusty ground, unable to locate Anna. He groped around for several minutes until his hand brushed the cord fastened to the back of her exosuit. He grabbed it tightly, wound the slack around his left hand then followed it, inching forward across the uneven ground. She was some distance from where she had disappeared, still crawling relentlessly towards the spacecraft. Unable to stand, she continued on her hands and knees, following the vague glow from the ground lights. They crawled blindly, one behind the other, finally reaching the bottom of Aeolis' landing strut. On all fours, they ascended the stairs until they located the airlock. Kenwyn gave five strong pulls on his rope, confirming they had made it. On receiving the signals, Kelly unclipped the lines from the dome, sending them whizzing into the storm.

Relieved to be inside, out of the maelstrom, Kenwyn pushed the lever up to re-pressurize the room. He looked over at her. Her visor had a huge crack running from top to bottom, just to the left of the midline.

'Can you hear me?' he asked.

'Yes,' she replied, their intercoms seamlessly patching into Aeolis' network.

'Are you okay?'

'Fine. Just a little shaken,' she said, taking off her helmet. 'It could've been a lot worse.'

'Looking at your helmet, it very nearly was.'

'Come on, we haven't got long.'

An intermittent siren resonated throughout the ship. Anna rushed down the narrow corridor towards the control room.

'That's the Reactor's pressure alarm, isn't it?' the medic asked.

'Yes. The radiation level seems to be okay at the moment,' she said, checking the meter on her suit.

An amber warning light flashed unrelentingly in the ceiling as they hurried down the narrow corridor in the center of the ship. Anna punched in her access code and the door slid open shortly afterwards. Without wasting any time, she sat down and switched on the computer monitor, swiftly initiating the status check program. She fidgeted nervously in the seat, waiting for the computer to run through its safety algorithms. Even though the room was poorly lit, Kenwyn saw the color drain from Anna's face as she muttered something under her breath in Russian.

'What is it?' he asked fearfully.

She ignored him, bringing up the feed from a camera in the reactor room. The caps covering the control rod assembly were jumping uncontrollably, the excess steam tossing them casually into the air.

'We have to get out of here!' she said animatedly. 'This ship is a massive bomb, and it's going to blow at any moment.'

'I don't understand. Surely we can fix it?'

'There's nothing we can do. It's past the point of no return. We haven't got time to discuss it. We have to go. NOW!'

They sprinted back through the ship, the onboard computer relaying verbal warnings over the ship's computer system.

'This kind of thing is meant to be impossible,' she said, breathing heavily. 'We have to get the Aeolis out of Mars' atmosphere before it explodes.'

'We'll need to talk to Kelly before we do that.'

'We don't have time!' she shouted, trying to be heard over the alarms.

Anna dropped into the seat in front of the Navigation Computer in the Communications Room.

'Computer, commence emergency launch procedure,' she said, raising her voice.

An acknowledgement rang out from the intercom speakers. The screen changed, a blue, glowing fingerprint appearing in the center of the display.

She held her index finger against the screen, impatiently waiting for the computer to identify her.

'Dr Anna Chernyakov recognized,' the computer announced after a few seconds, matching the voice with the fingerprint in its archives. 'Please enter your emergency override code.'

She tapped in a six-digit sequence, bringing up the Navigation screen. Moving through the options, her finger finally hovered over the escape vector icon.

'Ready?' she asked.

'Yes,'

Anna tapped the screen, initiating the countdown.

'Come on,' she screamed, running towards the airlock. 'We have two minutes to get as far away from this crate as possible.'

Fumbling with their helmets, they proceeded to decompress the small room.

'Is your helmet going to work with that crack in it'?

'I guess we're about to find out.'

Outside, they nimbly descended the steps. Once on solid ground, they held each other's hands, fleeing back into the storm.

17.

Kelly stood in the dome's airlock, still wearing her helmet and exosuit. Being outside was too dangerous, the swirling wind made it difficult to stay on her feet. She watched fretfully with one hand on the door handle, waiting for any sign of them.

Through the vast cloud, a brief flash illuminated the landscape, accompanied by a deep rumbling beneath her feet.

'The reactor's exploded,' she shouted, her panic evident for the rest of the crew to hear.

Wai and Tony faces reappeared in the corridor window, attempting to see what was happening.

'No, wait!' her voice changing to a mixture of relief and incredulity. 'It's the Aeolis' engines igniting.'

'You're kidding?' the assistant commander said incredulously over the intercom.

'What the hell are they playing at?' she mumbled to herself.

Kenwyn squeezed Anna's hand as they sprinted through the swirling dust, determined not to lose her this time. Once or twice, she lost her footing, but he tightened his grip, yanking her across the Martian surface. From behind them came a roar, the immense downward thrust from the engines shook the ground as the ship took off. The downdraft temporarily cleared the swirling clouds. As his field of view cleared, Kenwyn saw the lights of the dome momentarily to his right. Kelly spotted the two silhouettes and held the outer door open. Once they were safely inside, she slammed the door before raising the lever to re-pressurize the room. Finally, the light turned from red to green.

'What happened?' she demanded, ripping off her helmet.

'I had to initiate an emergency escape vector,' Anna said, gasping for breath. 'The Aeolis is lost. I had to get it out of the planet's atmosphere before the pressure vessel exploded.'

'Do you think it'll make it before it blows?'

'If it doesn't, it's irrelevant. We'll all be dead,' she said, her nonchalance incongruous.

Tony placed a tray of drinks on the table in front of them while the storm continued to whine outside.

'Can you explain to me what happened?' Wai asked. 'All I know is we had a problem with the reactor, and now we've lost the Aeolis.'

'I think the ship was struck by lightning,' she explained. 'Somehow, this caused an electrical fault so we couldn't slow the rate of energy production in the reactor. On top of that, it also stopped the pumps which circulate the water in the cooling system from working.'

'Basically, what you're saying is, the rate of reaction was racing out of control, and we couldn't stop it,' Tony summarized.

'Exactly. The heat from the fuel rods was making the steam in the containment vessel boil uncontrollably, causing the pressure inside the reactor to soar. It had gone too far. When I looked into the Reactor Room, the caps covering the fuel rods were dancing due to the high pressure beneath them. Each of them weighs several hundred kilograms, and they were jumping around like a paper boat on the sea. We only had a few minutes before it exploded, so to protect us and the planet, the only option was to sacrifice the Aeolis.'

'It sounds like the right decision,' Kelly said, sipping from her mug.

'With all this racket outside, how can we tell if the Aeolis has left the atmosphere in time?' asked Wai. 'The meters are off the scale in this storm anyway. For all we know, we could be being exposed to massive levels of radiation right now.'

'I've not felt any explosions,' Tony said. 'But I guess we're going to have to wait until the storm's passed or someone develops symptoms.'

'Kenwyn, what should we look out for?' Kelly asked.

'Normally, the first sign of radiation sickness is vomiting.' he said. 'So, I can't stress this enough, if any of you are sick, even once, you must tell me. Okay?'

Everyone nodded.

The next morning the conditions within the dome had not improved. The low temperature had led to ice forming on some of the interior walls. Gone were the t-shirts and flight suits, the five of them now wore everything they owned, looking like well-padded polar explorers.

Wai worked busily to stay warm, covering the seedlings in the greenhouse with horticultural fleece, protecting them from the cold.

'How are they bearing up?' Kelly asked, making her jump.

'There appears to be no harm done yet,' she said, her breath hanging in the air. 'But I can't be sure for a couple of days.'

'Is there anything I can do to help?'

'Not really, unless you can give me a few more degrees and some light. I can protect them from the cold; my worry is the darkness,' she said. 'If this goes on too long, the seedlings will become leggy. Ironically, the low temperatures will slow their growth down, which should help a little.'

Kelly looked up through the plexiglass roof. They were deep inside the swirling, red cloud. Outside, banks of red sand had formed against the side of the greenhouse and small rocks continually clattered as they rolled down the sloped walls.

'Terrifying, isn't it?' Wai said.

'I'm worried what Mac is going through,' Kelly said.

'I pray he made it to the Rover. He should be safe there.'

'I hope so.'

18.

Cramped inside the cab, it had been a highly unpleasant night. The ever-present sound of the buffeting wind accompanied Mac's ever thought. The storm showed no signs of abating and to make matters worse, the dashboard showed he had less than an hour of oxygen remaining. Over the last few hours, he had tried to sleep, but fear prevented him, so he sat motionless, trying to conserve as much energy as possible.

Scared and alone, he noticed it had become harder to take a deep enough breath, the air, seemingly, not reaching his lungs. He forced himself to take deeper, breaths but with little improvement.

'So, this is how it ends,' he thought to himself.

Having been one of the first people to set foot on Mars, he had achieved a lot, but he was not ready to die. There was still so much he wanted to do. Nonetheless, if this was how he was going to die, it was out of his hands. He hated the passivity of waiting for his life to ebb away and for death to take hold.

His breathing quickly became labored, and his vision began to close in. He replaced his helmet, opened the dividing door and laid down on one of the benches in the back of the Rover. The additional oxygen from his suit restored his sight, and his respiration settled.

The next couple of hours passed slowly, but he knew it was futile. He briefly toyed with the idea of walking out into the storm and removing his helmet, to avoid putting off the inevitable, but death would come soon enough as the oxygen dial on his left wrist visibly dropped with each breath. An unfamiliar alarm began chirping, accompanied by an orange LED flashing inside his helmet. Over the next thirty minutes, the periphery of his vision shrank away, leaving only monochrome, slow-motion images. His thoughts became interwoven with dreams, his awareness beginning to drift away.

Someone entered the vehicle, the Rover rocking as the door slammed shut. A voice spoke, calling him by name. It was someone he had heard before, but not instantly familiar.

'This must be death,' he thought with diminishing clarity.

The voice spoke again, the tone calm, almost welcoming. Mac felt his helmet being removed but was powerless to resist as he continued to drift towards unconsciousness. What little lucidity remained, warped into a twisted dream before everything turned black.

***

The storm had continued into its third day. No one had slept well. Their current situation was so horrendous the crew kept themselves locked away in their individual quarters. Realistically, there was no way Mac could have survived this long. They knew his oxygen supply would have run out more than twelve hours ago.

Kelly put her pillow over her head, trying to block the continual groaning from the storm. As commander, she was responsible for the wellbeing of her crew, and Mac being caught out on his own was entirely her fault. Certainly, that is how the Agency would see it. It was hard to believe he was dead. He was the most jovial member of the team, always looking on the bright side of any situation and adapting to life without him was going to be tough. She would have to support the others through the complex emotions which grief brought, but on top of that, she would have to push them even harder, so the colony would be ready for the arrival of the Discovery.

After several hours of restless anxiety, Kelly gave up on the idea of sleeping. Wandering towards the Dining Room, she spotted Tony, standing in the airlock, staring out into the swirling madness. His gaze was fixed on the storm. He pulled the blanket he was wearing tighter around his shoulders, his nose still pressed against the glass.

'Where is he?' she heard the assistant commander whisper.

'Have you been here all night,' Kelly said. 'You'll catch your death of cold standing in here.'

Tony turned around instinctively but quickly looked away.

'I'm not here to fight. I've brought a peace offering,' she said, handing him a hot mug of coffee.

'I thought we had no power.'

'We don't,' she said. 'But I turned the dome's heating off for two minutes so I could make this for you.'

'Thanks,' he said, cradling it in his cold, white hands.

He sipped tentatively at the mug's contents, continuing to stare through the giant window.

'I'm sorry,' he said without making eye contact. 'The way I spoke to you wasn't fair. You didn't deserve that.'

'Apology accepted,' she said with a smile which went unseen. 'Mac's lucky to have a friend like you.'

'I feel so helpless.'

'We all do.'

They stood together, staring out through the window, their minds lost in the dust cloud.

'Come on, it's freezing in here,' she said, leading him into the corridor with her arm around his shoulders.

'How's your stomach? Is the wound giving you any issues?'

'Only occasional twinges,' he said. 'It's much better, thanks.'

'Great,' she said. 'When the storm's passed, and all this has settled, I'm going to need you to start fabricating panels to extend the dome in preparation for the arrival of the Discovery.'

'How long do we have?'

'Only a couple of weeks, I'm afraid,' she said. 'If we're not finished, it will get pretty cramped in here. There is barely enough room for us, let alone another hundred colonists.'

'Kenwyn says I'm not allowed to do any heavy lifting at the moment,' he tried to explain.

'Don't worry about that,' the medic said, making them both jump. 'That's what I'm here for. We just need you to fabricate the panels.'

'Okay,' he replied. 'We can start when Mac gets back.'

Unseen by Tony, Kelly shot Kenwyn a nervous glance.

Hearing voices, Anna cocooned herself in her bedclothes and padded her way into the Dining Room, the icy floor cold under her bare feet.

'Couldn't sleep either, huh?' the commander said.

'Nope. It's pointless to even try while this continues.'

Kelly made her a cup of coffee with the remaining warm water.

Anna took a sip before speaking, 'Have any of you had any funny experiences recently?'

'How do you mean?' Kelly asked.

'It seems kind of silly, but I keep having this strange feeling someone's watching me. I've experienced it ever since we arrived. You know, it's that feeling you get when someone stares at you, but when I've turned around, there's no one there.'

'I can't say I have,' said Kenwyn.

'I thought I saw someone up on the ridge the

other day, but when I looked back, they'd gone,' Kelly said.

'I haven't seen anything,' Tony said. 'But I've hardly left the dome.'

'I've not spoken about it before,' Anna said. 'But it's really creeping me out at the moment.'

19.

Over the previous twelve hours, the clouds had become visibly thinner. Tony continued his vigil in the airlock, desperate to glimpse Mac or the Rover.

'The power's up to seventy percent,' Kelly announced over the dome's intercom. 'Hopefully, it means the worst is over.'

'I hope we can turn the heating back on and stop dressing like this,' Wai said, still wearing a woolly hat and gloves.

'Maybe in an hour or so,' Anna said, looking at the dials on the wall. 'Let's give the batteries a chance to store some charge.'

'When are we going to look for Mac,' asked Tony.

Kenwyn pressed stared through the glass, before pressing the button on the intercom, 'I think we're safe to go out,' he said. 'It looks a bit windier than usual, but we should be okay.'

A smile broadened across Tony's face.

'All right let's suit up and get out there,' the commander said. 'But Tony, I want you to stay here and keep trying him on the radio.'

'I need to help look for him,' he protested, his face darkening. 'I feel fine now.'

'You've only just recovered from abdominal surgery. You need to remain here,' Kenwyn insisted.

'I can't sit here and do nothing,' he said. 'I feel so useless.'

'It'll be fine,' said Kelly, appearing in the doorway. 'We'll keep the channel open, and you can listen to the chatter.'

From the corridor, Tony watched forlornly as Kelly, Anna and Kenwyn put their helmets on. As the last man out, the medic gave a wave before stepping through the external airlock door.

'Gosh! I've never seen the crater without the Aeolis.' Anna said.

'It feels weird, doesn't it?' said Kenwyn.

'Let's head out to the pods,' Kelly said. 'That's where he was when the storm came in but spread out, we don't want to miss anything.'

Vast banks of red sand partially submerged the dome. Walking was more difficult. The three of them sinking up to their knees in the drifts which now occupied the landscape. Stopping every couple of hundred yards, they searched for signs of Mac. Kenwyn scoured the horizon with the magnifier held up to the visor of his helmet. Meanwhile, they could hear Tony trying to contact Mac on the intercom.

On reaching the cargo site, Kelly and Anna set about digging around the three metal structures with their gloved hands to allow them to open them.

One by one, they opened the massive doors of the

pods, afraid of what they might find inside.

'Nothing,' the medic said, letting out an exasperated sigh, looking inside the final pod.

'Mac?' Kelly cried desperately into the microphone in her helmet. 'Come in, Mac?'

No reply.

'Over here!' said Anna with a tinge of excitement in her voice.

Kenwyn and Kelly attempted to run over to where she was standing, but the dust made it little more than an awkward trudge.

'I've found some of the Rover's tire tracks,' she said, pointing to the remains of two parallel channels near her feet. 'But they're heading in completely the wrong direction.'

'He must have been disorientated by the storm,' Kelly said. 'Come on, we've only got an hour before our radiation monitors time out.'

'That means we can only follow the tracks for around a quarter of an hour,' Kenwyn said. 'Fifteen minutes out, fifteen minutes back and then another thirty to make it back to the dome.'

'Roger that,' Kelly said. 'Tony, can you keep an eye on the clock? Let us know when fifteen minutes are up.'

'Will do,' he said.

They scoured the ground, looking for the remnants of the tire tracks among the banks of dust. Where they disappeared, they spread out and searched until they found them again.

'This isn't going to be good news,' Anna said. 'He's a long way from home with little oxygen left.'

'Let's deal with what we find,' Kelly said, keenly aware Tony was listening. 'Mac's quite resourceful.'

'Hey, over here,' said Kenwyn, a hundred meters ahead of them.

'What is it?' the commander asked, running to him.

'The dust pattern is unusual. It's similar to the size and shape of the Rover's chassis.'

The three of them stood around a rectangular depression surrounded by mounds of red sand deposited around the edges.

'It looks like he stopped here for quite some time,' said Anna.

'Is that a footprint?' Kenwyn asked.

'it's hard to say,' Kelly stated. 'Mac's not stupid enough to leave the Rover in such a bad storm, he's smarter than that.'

'I guess so, but where's the Rover?'

'That's the million-dollar question,' said Anna.

'Unfortunately, your fifteen minutes is up,' Tony's voice appearing in their headsets.

'Thanks, Tony. We're heading back now,' the commander said. 'Kenwyn, see if there are any signs of him on the horizon.'

The medic held the magnifier up and slowly turned through three-hundred and sixty degrees.

'Nothing,' he said, disappointment obvious in his voice.'

'Okay,' said Kelly. 'Let's move out.'

'Tell me what you found,' Tony said, bursting into the airlock as soon as the light had changed color. 'It was hard to follow what was happening over the intercom.'

'We may have located the Rover's tracks, but nothing else,' Kelly said, tying her hair back after taking off her helmet.

'What was that about a footprint?' he persisted. 'You mentioned footprints.'

'There's a rectangular area in the middle of some sand drifts. It's about the same size as the Rover,' Kelly tried to explain. 'Beside it, we found a smaller depression in the bank of dust, it could be a footprint, but it could equally be just a mark left by the storm.'

'We went as far as we could,' Kenwyn repeated. 'If those depressions are tracks from the Rover, and it still is only if, then he was heading in the wrong direction.'

'Let's go straight back out after the cool-off period,' Wai proposed, trying to be helpful. 'We can go further if we walk straight to the last point we reached.'

'Okay,' Kelly agreed. 'Wai, Kenwyn and Anna, go back outside when the radiation break is over. In the meantime, get yourselves a drink.'

'I think I should go,' Tony said forcibly.

'We've been through this,' Kelly said, struggling to remain calm. 'You're not well enough.'

The assistant commander continued to beg, his eyes pleading for her to let him go with the others.

'No,' the medic said finally. 'I'm sorry, but you're not fit. You'd slow us down. It's better for Mac if you stay here.'

He glared at them before stomping out.

Once she had waved goodbye to the three people heading outside, Kelly returned to her quarters and recorded a video message for the Agency, explaining about the storm, the loss of the Aeolis and a crew

135

member missing, presumed dead. Trying to avoid a long list of woes, she neglected to mention the rapidly deteriorating relationship between her and her second in command.

Lying face down on her bed, tears began to well in her eyes. Many emotions swirled around her head. From the moment she opened her eyes every morning until she closed them at night, self-doubt seemed to occupy her every thought. It was paralyzing. She felt such a failure, unsure how things could be worse.

She was woken by Kenwyn's voice over the dome's intercom, requesting her presence in the Dining Room. She struggled to the edge of the bunk, letting out a lethargic yawn. Catching a glimpse of herself in the mirror opposite, she was repulsed by what she saw. Dark rings had formed beneath her eyes, and her skin looked dull and pallid. Scraping her hair back into a greasy ponytail, she rinsed the traces of tears from her face. She straightened her uniform, assessing her appearance carefully. Mars was taking its toll on all of them.

When she entered the room, most of her remaining crew were sitting around the table. Wai was absent, but occasionally visible in the airlock, refilling everyone's air tanks.

'How far did you get?' Kelly asked.

'We were able to go much further this time,' Kenwyn answered. 'But there's still no sign of Mac or the Rover.'

'The tracks drop down into a valley and continue way beyond the range we can cover on foot,' the botanist said.

'We went straight to where we left off last time,' the medic said. 'We can't go any further.'

'Thanks for trying,' the commander said.

'What? That's it?' Tony snapped. 'You're giving up, just like that?'

'What else can we do?' Kelly said, her frustration audible in her voice.

'This is ridiculous,' he exclaimed. 'It's as if you don't care about him. You were willing to risk your lives for the reactor.'

'That was different,' Anna jumped in. 'If the reactor had blown, we would have all been vaporized.'

'Tony, we all care about Mac,' Kelly said, trying hard to remain calm. 'But we can't put anyone else at risk. The colony must be ready for when the Discovery arrives.'

'Now, the truth surfaces,' he shouted. 'You're writing him off because your husband's nearly here.'

'Tony!' Kenwyn scolded. 'That's out of order.'

'This would not have happened if I'd been in command,' Tony ranted, now standing up. 'We both know it should have been me. You might have more hours than me in the simulator, but I've had considerably more time in space than you.'

Kelly refused to break eye contact with him but said nothing.

'Your appointment was purely tokenism,' he continued angrily. 'The Agency wanted a woman to lead the mission, not the most qualified person. It wouldn't surprise me if you've slept your way into the position.'

She bit her tongue, avoiding saying something regrettable. Eventually, she replied in a forced, calculated tone through tight lips, 'I will not put any other member of my crew in harm's way.'

'It's a bit late for that. You killed Mac.' he bellowed before overturning his chair and stomping out of the room.

'Well, that's a nice welcome back,' Anna said. 'Are you okay?'

'I'm fine,' she lied, clearly shaken by the confrontation.

Anna, Kenwyn and Kelly crowded around a map on the table in the Operations Room. First, they located the crater, circling their current position and the coordinates of the cargo pods then plotted their route and the approximate location where they thought the Rover had stopped.

'Well, there's not a lot out there,' Kenwyn said, standing back from the map.

'We have to assume he's dead,' said Kelly glumly as Wai entered the room. 'His oxygen couldn't last this long.'

'There must be some hope,' the botanist said, pulling up a chair.

'Not unless you believe in miracles. It's been more than twenty-four hours.'

'It doesn't seem fair,' Wai said. 'To survive all we've been through, then to die in a storm like that.'

'It's no one's fault, but it really sucks,' said Kenwyn. 'He was just too far from safety when the storm began.'

'It's given us one hell of a wake-up call,' Kelly said. 'We've been too casual about being on the surface. We need to be more careful. Given a chance, the planet will seize any opportunity to kill us.'

***

'That woman is messing with my head,' Tony said, sitting on the edge of Wai's bed.

'She's just doing her job,' she replied objectively. 'It can't be easy for her.'

'This is the most important mission in human history and her decision-making over the last few days suggests she's not up to it.'

'The Agency selected Kelly as commander,' she reasoned. 'She's very talented.'

'I'll tell you what she is,' said Tony, becoming angry. 'She's a symbolic gesture. They wanted a woman to command this mission just to achieve some arbitrary diversity quota.'

'That's an awful thing to say.'

'It's true, you look at our records. I have twice as many flight hours as her, and I've been commander on many more space flights. She's only here because she's a woman.'

'She does seem to have buried Mac before we've found a body.'

'Infuriating, isn't it? We should do something about it.'

'What can we do?'

'We take control ourselves! We only need one of the others to come around to our way of thinking to give us a majority, then we can take over without force.'

'Tony, what you're talking about is mutiny!'

'No. It's not. It's relieving her of command

because she's incompetent.'

'You can't be serious.'

'I absolutely am,' he said. 'Directive one-three-six states the second in command may take temporary charge if the mental state of the commanding officer has deteriorated to such an extent it threatens the mission objectives or the safety of the crew.'

'I'm not sure what happened to Mac was the result of deterioration in Kelly's mental health.'

'You heard it yourself. Kelly said she would not put any other member of her crew in harm's way. So, in my mind, she's admitting it was her fault.'

20.

A network of wind turbines, with their feverishly rotating broad, steel blades, now marked the perimeter of the rapidly, expanding colony. These would provide the additional power required to support the colonists after they landed. Tony and Kenwyn had toiled relentlessly to build a Fabrication Centre adjacent to the dome. The pyramidal structure, enclosing a bare dirt floor, now towered above their home. Anna had tapped into the dome's environmental systems, giving the new facility electricity, breathable air and climate control. As the arrival of the Discovery approached, work now occupied every minute of their days. Dinner became the only occasion throughout the day when everyone met together.

Tony sank his spade into the dusty ground, transferring its contents to the hopper on the giant 3-D fabricator then flicked the small, red switch on the back of the machine. Its casing vibrated as giant rotors began mixing the dust with gallons of water, producing a thick, muddy paste. After a few minutes, a graceful robotic arm began following a predefined program, depositing blobs of the reddy-brown sludge, slowly bringing a wall panel into being.

'This one's nearly done,' Tony called across the high-ceilinged room.

'Thanks, I'll move it shortly,' Kenwyn replied, taking a loaded trolley out of the kiln. He probed the consistency of freshly baked panels, 'These seem ready to be used.'

'Great, they're for the new residential block.'

'Excellent. We're going to have to make a lot more before its finished.'

'Well, if there's one thing we have, it's plenty of dust,' the medic said.

The two men worked in the hot and gritty environment, digging and mixing as they prepared the materials for numerous panels.

'There's still no sign of him,' the medic said gently.

Tony screwed up his face, looking away.

'I think he tried to reach us on foot,' Tony said eventually, admitting for the first time Mac was dead. 'We'll probably find his body buried somewhere.'

'I guess you're right. It's awful. I miss him so much.'

'Me too. I still think she gave up looking for him too early,' Tony said, refusing to even say Kelly's name.

'The storm went on for too long. Mac would have run out of oxygen long before we got to him.'

'I wanted to go, but you and Kelly stopped me,' he replied, failing to hide his anger. 'Maybe I would have reached him in time.'

'Tony, you've got to be realistic; we would have

ended up with two funerals, maybe more.'

'We don't know that. Perhaps he found a way of extending his oxygen supply.'

'You're clutching at straws. Where would he have found oxygen on Mars?'

'He's a resourceful chap.'

'Only if he's able to manufacture it out of nothing.'

***

As the commander, Kelly had the responsibility of conducting the memorial service for Mac. Without a coffin, it was going to be hard for anyone to find closure. She was particularly dreading Tony's reaction. Things were still sour between them, and the ceremony would only amplify the raw emotions.

Wearing her navy-blue ceremonial uniform, she walked reluctantly to the Ops Room, her white cap with its gold braid under her arm. She had last worn this for the official photoshoot before they left Earth. Nausea welled up inside her, causing her to pause in the doorway. The rest of them, dressed in similar attire, waited as soft, emotive music played over the dome's speaker system. At the front of the room, a saltire, the flag of Mac's native Scotland, lay on her desk. Kelly swallowed hard, clearing the taste of bile from her mouth. After taking a deep breath, she placed her cap on her head, pulling the black peak level with her eyebrows.

Striding up the aisle, she took her place at the front of the room and faced the crew, her legs touching the table.

'Please take your seats,' she said, with an uncomfortable politeness.

Tony and Wai sat on one side of the central aisle, Kenwyn and Anna on the other, their solemn faces focusing on her.

'We are gathered here to say farewell to Lieutenant Michael MacDonald to commit him into the hands of God,' Kelly began, her voice cracking.

'What can I say about Mac?' she said, looking around the room. 'When I think of him, I can only smile. He was so full of life. He exuded a kind of infectious energy; you could not avoid being cheered up by him. Everything he did, was done with enthusiasm, not to mention his terrible singing,' her comments prompting a few smiles.

'I first met him back at the Agency. It must have been around five years ago at the start of the selection process for this mission,' she continued. 'In the relatively short time, I knew him, it was clear he lived life to its fullest and clearly loved it. His most endearing feature was his uncomplicated personality. He had the excitement of a child and found enjoyment in the small things. I can think of many stories, too many to fit into one speech, but I'm sure you agree, being around him was a blessing and our lives were richer for knowing him. I miss him, he was my friend, and my heart longs to see him again.'

She paused to compose herself, blinking back tears.

'Lord God, you are the source of life. In you we live,' she read from the Agency's order of service. 'Keep us in your love. By your grace, lead us to your kingdom through Jesus Christ, your son. In the Name of God, the merciful Father, we entrust the body of

Michael MacDonald into your hands until you raise him up on the last day. Receive him into your peace. Amen.'

As previously arranged, Kenwyn started a recording of a single piper playing a Scottish lament. Kelly fixed her eyes on the flag laying on the table while the mournful music played, tears running freely.

When the music stopped, her white-gloved hand hovered to the right side of her face as she formally saluted the flag. The other crew members reciprocated in silence. She looked at each of them, their heartfelt emotions unashamedly visible. Wai comforted Tony as he cried uncontrollably, his face red and crumpled.

21.

Kelly tapped the access code into the keyboard, waiting impatiently for the connection to establish. She rested back in her chair as the call connected.

The screen came to life with a fuzzy picture of Ryan.

'How are you?' she said once the image and sound had synchronized.

'Better now,' he said with relief visible on his face.

'What do you mean? Better how?'

'It's been awful. We've had an outbreak of some kind of virus on the ship. Two of the colonists are dead, and we still have fifteen in quarantine.'

'That's terrible. Were you ill?'

'No, but when there's something like this on board, you over analyze every headache.'

'It sounds horrendous. When did all start?'

'About a month after we launched. Our medics think one of the colonists must have had it when they boarded.'

'At least it's something from Earth, not some

weird space virus. Do you know what caused it?'

'Before we left communications range, I spent many hours on video conferences with our Chief Medical Officer and the Agency. They've come to the conclusion it's something called Hantavirus. To be honest, I'd never heard of it.'

'Me neither. What are the symptoms, so I can tell Kenwyn what to look out for down here?'

'In the beginning, it feels like the flu. Patients seem to start with a high temperature, then a cough which, from what I saw, progressed quickly to severe breathlessness and then death within a few days.'

'Sounds ghastly. Where does this leave us with the colony?'

'Apparently, the incubation period can be as long as a month, so I guess we have to stay onboard the Discovery for four weeks after the last person has recovered.'

'Are you going to land or remain in orbit?'

'The Agency insist we keep off the planet until this has fully resolved to maintain biosecurity.'

'I think that's the right thing to do, but it's going to be hard knowing you're so near, but I can't see you.'

'Yeah,' Ryan smiled with an air of resignation. 'They say we're going to be up here for another few weeks. The good news is all astronauts have been routinely vaccinated against it, so we're all okay. For some reason, no one considered vaccinating the colonists.'

'Don't tell me, cost-saving exercise?'

'Yep, you're a mind reader.'

'What's happened to those who died?' she asked. 'Are they in cold storage?'

'No, the Agency didn't want the risk of introducing

the disease to Mars, so they instructed us to conduct space burials.'

'You mean jettisoning their bodies?' she asked incredulously.

'Yeah, such a sad end. We held a small ceremony of remembrance for those who were well enough to attend.'

'How many people have caught the virus?'

'None of the crew, but most of the colonists. From what I can tell, there are two types of this illness,' he said. 'A mild, self-limiting form, which is like the flu. It only lasts for a few days and then resolves. On the other hand, the exceptionally aggressive kind causes multi-organ failure and patients deteriorate quickly. Thankfully, the majority of cases have been the less severe variety.'

'That's good, I guess.'

'Unfortunately, those who are currently sick have the bad type. The medical staff are not expecting many of them to pull through.'

'Is there any chance those who have recovered will relapse?'

'The medics don't think so. But to be honest, no one's sure.'

'Great,' she said sarcastically. 'Anyway, how are you holding up? From the sounds of it, you've had a stressful flight.'

'I'm just relieved to be here.'

'You look exhausted.' Her voice heavy with concern.

'I may not be looking my best, but don't worry, I'm fine. How are things down on the surface?'

'A little tense,' she said reluctantly. 'Mac died in a dust storm, and Tony blames me.'

'Mac's dead?' The shock catching in his voice. 'I can't believe it.'

'I'm struggling to get my head around it myself. He was caught outside when a storm appeared out of nowhere. Presumably, he ran out of oxygen before we could get to him. We've not found his body or the Rover though.'

'That's odd. Can you be sure he's dead?'

'He was trying to find the dome, but with the visibility being so poor, it looks like he drove off in the wrong direction. The tracks lead beyond the limit we can cover on foot.'

'I guess all will become clear once the Discovery's Rovers are down on the surface. What did you say about Tony blaming you?'

'He wanted to go out in the middle of the storm and search for Mac.'

'But that would be crazy.'

'I know, but he won't listen.'

'How's the rest of your team?'

'Okay, considering what we've been through. With Mac gone and Tony not at full capacity, we're a little behind schedule.'

'The schedule is the least of your worries. How's Tony doing?'

'He's improving physically, but he seems all over the place emotionally.'

'Have patience with him, he's been through a lot. You all have.'

'When you do finally touch down, the colonists and your crew will have to stay on the Discovery until the accommodation block is finished.'

'It's going to be a little cramped on the landing pad with both the Aeolis and us down there.'

'The Aeolis has gone,' she said.

'What? I thought it wasn't scheduled to go for another couple of weeks,' he said, slightly puzzled.

'I have so much to tell you,' she said, tucking a loose strand of hair behind her ear. 'It took damage during the storm, making the reactor overheat. Anna had to launch it to avoid it exploding on the planet. Apparently, there was nothing she could do to save the reactor. Surface radiation levels haven't spiked, so the ship must have blown up outside the atmosphere.'

'Hell!' he exclaimed. 'I'll check our data. Do you have any cheerful news from Mars?' he said with a wry smile.

'Not really. The last few weeks have been pretty full-on.'

'It sounds that way, but it won't be long until I'm with you,' he said reassuringly.

'I can't wait.' Her face lighting up. 'At least your delay gives us a chance to make good headway on the accommodation block.

'Another couple of days on this crate shouldn't matter after the journey we've had. As soon as all signs of the virus have gone, we can help out with the construction.'

A female voice crackled over the dome's intercom, 'Kelly, I need you in the Ops Room.'

'Gotta go. Wai wants something.'

'Okay, Let's catch up later. Love you.'

'Love you too.'

'What is it?' Kelly said anxiously, hurrying through the door.

'I hope you don't mind me calling you, but I have

something I'd like you to see.'

Kelly pulled up a chair, her eyes fixed on the botanist.

'I've been flying one of Mac's surveillance drone, following what's left of the Rover's tire tracks to see if I can locate it,' Wai said.

'Good idea, but I thought Mac was using the drones when he was out in the storm.'

'He never repaired the damaged one, so I fixed it, with a little help from Tony.'

'Okay,' the commander said, slightly too defensively. 'What have you found?'

'Watch,' said Wai, fiddling with the controls, bringing up a grainy video image on the big screen.

'We know the tracks headed away from the dome,' she explained, showing images of an area Kelly recognized, the strange depression in the ground, where they had suspected the Rover had stopped during the storm. 'So, I flew the drone along the same heading,' Wai continued, speeding up the clip.

The two of them watched as the camera passed through regions Kelly had never seen before.

'The trail was understandably patchy in places, and it was incredibly hard to follow at times,' Wai said. 'But I lost the trail here. After that, I couldn't find any trace of him.'

The screen showed a path descending into a dusty gully. A rocky cliff on the left of the image had been violently torn away, littering the ground with large, beige boulders.

'Okay,' said Kelly, somewhat puzzled. 'What does this tell us?'

'On its own, nothing, but the area we're looking at is only a mile from the remains of the Erebus. I was wondering if this is what the ship hit when Earth lost contact with her.'

'Could be. Do you think Mac accidentally stumbled onto the crash site?' she asked, not sure where this conversation was going.

'It's a long shot, but maybe he made it to the wreck, and he's taking shelter there.'

'Wai, that's a little far-fetched,' Kelly said, her comments visibly causing disappointment. 'We know, the Erebus was destroyed on impact. We've all seen the satellite images.'

'Actually, all we've seen is the debris field. Some of the superstructure remains relatively intact. It's not implausible he could be there.'

'I understand what you're saying, but it's unlikely the ship's reactor survived that kind of impact. The radiation leak alone would render it uninhabitable.'

'Perhaps,' Wai said. 'But we can't be sure. Our sensors haven't detected any evidence of that on the surface. That would explain why we can't find any sign of Mac or the Rover.'

'Why did you stop here? Could you not fly the drone over the crash site? That would answer the question definitively.'

'I was searching for tire tracks, and hovering uses up a lot of battery power. They're currently recharging, so I should be ready to try again tomorrow.'

'How long do you think it would take us to walk there?'

'Around four or five hours.'

'Imagine the radiation exposure from being out there for that long. I'm sorry, but there's not enough evidence to send anyone on such a hazardous journey, just on the off-chance Mac is sheltering in the Erebus which miraculously survived the crash.'

'But...,' Wai tried to protest.

'No,' Kelly said forcibly. 'We'll have to wait until the Discovery lands. Then we can use one of their Rovers to check this out.'

'Perhaps he's injured. We could help him.'

'There are too many what-ifs. All we know for certain is the Rover was heading in completely the wrong direction. There's been no positive sighting of him or the vehicle. Until I am sure he's at the Erebus, I am not going to risk the life of anyone else on a wild goose chase, is that clear?'

'How can you sit here if there's a chance he's still alive.'

'Wai, I appreciate all you've done, but we have no other option.'

***

The emotionally charged atmosphere hung heavily. Unspoken words had been replaced by suspicious, furtive glances. At dinner, Tony and Wai chose to sit at a small table, separate from their colleagues, the lack of conversation adding to the unpleasantness.

'I have some news,' Kelly said, standing up after finishing her food. 'The Discovery has arrived in geostationary orbit above us.'

'Excellent, do they land tomorrow?' Anna asked.

'No. They've had an outbreak of something called Hantavirus. The whole ship's in quarantine.'

'How long before they touch down?' asked Wai,

looking back over her shoulder towards Kelly. 'With their Rovers, we can explore the Erebus crash site.'

'The current estimate is a couple of weeks. The Agency said the disease has to burn itself out first.'

'Two weeks!' exclaimed Wai.

'Are they certain it's Hantavirus?' Kenwyn asked. 'That's usually spread by mice.'

'They think one of the colonists had the infection when they boarded the Discovery, just they weren't demonstrating any symptoms at that point.'

'Is it serious?' Anna said, her voice heavy with concern.

'Occasionally, it can cause multi-organ failure,' the medic said. 'But most of the time, no. Patients just feel lousy for a few days.'

'They've had several deaths already,' Kelly added.

'How awful. Those poor people,' Wai said.

'So, are we at any risk?' Tony asked, his tone dismissive.

'No, we've all been vaccinated against it,' Kenwyn said, much to everyone's relief. 'It was part of the cocktail of jabs they gave us back on Earth. To be on the safe side, we should adopt a strict biosecurity protocol when they finally do land. We have to protect any potential life on this planet. We don't know the impact it would have if it encountered a virus like that.'

'Good idea, and if infected mice are hiding on the Discovery, those measures will prevent them from getting into the dome or the accommodation blocks.'

'Any news on the sick colonists?' the medic asked, returning his attention to the commander.

'Apparently, most are recovering, but a few are still critical and not expected to survive.'

'More people she's going to allow to die,' Tony whispered, loud enough for the commander to hear.

'Do you want to say something, Tony?' Kelly snapped.

He smiled sardonically, 'I was asking how much of a threat this virus is to us?'

'Virtually none,' Kenwyn said. 'Like I said, all astronauts are routinely vaccinated for it.'

'In the meantime, we need to prepare for their arrival,' Kelly said. 'Tony, I need you and Kenwyn to finish fabricating and assembling the wall panels. The other buildings will have to wait. Let's get everything in place so we can connect the accommodation block to the power and utilities. Wai, what's the status of the secondary greenhouses?'

As Wai began speaking, the water in the glass in front of her slopped unexpectedly onto the table. Puzzled, she stared at it, uncertain why this had happened. The ground started shaking, lightly at first but quickly rising to a crescendo. Through the door, she watched as the screen on the Ops Room wall crashed to the floor.

'What's happening?' Anna screamed.

'Perhaps the Discovery's landing,' Wai shouted, trying to make herself heard.

'No, it's an earthquake,' Tony yelled. 'Everyone, get under the tables, now!'

22.

Everyday objects became airborne as they huddled together under the table. The dome creaked wildly as the ground rippled beneath them. One of the interior wall panels clattered to the floor, landing inches from where they sheltered. Suddenly, they felt a distant thud followed by an explosion-like blast which seemed to suck the air out of the room. The lights went out, and an intermittent, red warning beacon began flashing accompanied by a high-pitched siren. The steel door between the Dining Room and the corridor leading to the greenhouse closed automatically.

'It's the pressure alarm,' Anna screamed.

Kelly crawled out and struggled to her feet. Bouncing off the furniture, she made her way towards the small computer screen which hung precariously on the wall. The lights went out, and something fell, glancing the side of her head, knocking her down. She clambered back up, blood trickling from the wound on her temple. Steadying herself, she flicked through several screens, searching for the cause of the alert. The list was long, but only one had a warning triangle next to it.

'Quick, put your suits on,' Kelly shouted over the rumbling earthquake. 'There's a breach in the outer wall. We're going to be out of air soon.'

The crew leapt out from their shelter and sprinted towards the airlock where the exosuits were stored, navigating the undulating floor while the tremor continued. Kelly counted them as they moved past her. One of the crew was missing. They had all been together in the dining room, so where were they? Her eyes scoured the Dining Room frantically until she made out something moving in the light emanating from the screen. Petrified, Wai cowered beneath the table, tears streaming down her panicked face. Crawling beside her, Kelly put her arm around the botanist, her slight frame quivering in her embrace.

'We're going to be okay,' the commander said, raising her voice to be heard. 'But we can't stay here.'

'I'm scared,' Wai said, barely audible above the uproar.

'I am too, but we have to leave.'

The air was beginning to feel thinner, each breath requiring more effort. Kelly helped the botanist to her feet before ushering her over the bulkhead into the corridor. Sealing the heavy, metal door behind them, the commander turned to find the airlock in disarray, the remaining exosuits, helmets and equipment lay scattered across the floor. After slipping into her suit, she deftly attached the portable oxygen supply before putting on her helmet. Once she was sure everyone was safe, her heart rate began to settle.

'Let's stay in here 'til it's over,' she said over the

intercom in her headset.

Guided by the lights in their helmets, Kelly led them through into the darkness of the Operations Room. Her suit's respirator hissed as she surveyed the devastation; the dome's interior was in chaos. The red emergency beacon cycled on relentlessly as the crew set about restore the contents of the room.

After clearing debris from the desk and rearranging her computer, Kelly used it to locate the pressure leak. It had originated in their sleeping quarters, the rest of the structure appeared unaffected. Opening the security menu, she isolated their sleeping quarters; triggering the sound of the internal, steel doors slamming shut throughout the dome. Next, she turned off the air supply to the damaged section of the structure and instructed the computer to shut down the climate controls in that area. Now the leak had been isolated, she tapped in a code which recommenced the re-pressurization of the portions which remained habitable.

While waiting for the air to become breathable again, Kelly and her crewmates continued to tidy the rooms they still had access to. It took several hours before, the red light stopped flashing, and the siren ceased.

'I guess we're spending the night in here,' Anna observed, taking off her helmet.

'Yep, better make yourselves comfortable,' Kelly said. 'Tomorrow, we'll have to go outside and inspect the damage.'

'How's your head?' Kenwyn asked.

'It's fine,' the commander shrugged nonchalantly.

'Let me look,' he said, probing the wound with his fingers. 'It'll need a couple of stitches.'

A low, repetitive bell interrupted them.

'What's that?' Tony asked. 'I don't recognize that alarm.'

'Don't worry,' said Kelly. 'That's not an alarm, it's an incoming call.'

She leant over the desk, pressing the answer button on the desktop, bringing the screen which lay on the floor to life.

'Kelly, thank God,' said Ryan. 'Our sensors picked up an earthquake on the surface. Is everyone okay?'

'Part of the dome has depressurized, but we're all fine.'

'How bad is it?'

'It only appears to be the sleeping quarters, but we'll get a better idea in the morning when we can have a closer look.'

'What's happened to your head?' her husband asked, noticing the wound.

'Don't worry, it's only a scratch.'

'Let me know if there are any aftershocks. It would be breaking protocol, but we could descend and evacuate if needed.'

'Thanks, I suspect it's going to be a long night, but I think we're okay. I'd better go. Bye.'

Tony and Wai quickly set about examining the habitable parts of the dome for any structural integrity issues, while Kenwyn and Anna inspected the environmental systems. In the generator room, the Russian engineer lay with her head underneath the primary power coupling which connected the

159

incoming cables from the solar panels and windmills to the energy storage unit.

'Can you hand me that?' she said to the medic, pointing at the row of tools she had laid out.

'This?' the medic asked, holding up an adjustable wrench.

'Yep. A few of the bolts have worked loose. It's a good job it didn't disconnect completely. It could have easily caused a fire.'

'I'm so glad it didn't. We've had enough drama since we arrived here.'

'Do you think all the issues we've had are a sign we shouldn't be here?' she said after a pause.

'How do you mean?'

'Well, we've had nothing but problems,' she said, straining as she tightened the coupling. 'Tony's illness, the reactor, what happened to Mac and now this. Perhaps someone's trying to tell us something.'

'Someone?' You don't strike me as someone who believes in God.'

'I'm not, but so many bad things have happened. It's as if the planet doesn't want us here.'

'We knew Mars was a hostile place before we left.'

'But I keep wondering, what else is going to go wrong?'

'You can't think like that.'

'I can't help it. I don't want to die here.'

'One day you will, but hopefully not soon.'

'What happened to Mac makes you think, though, doesn't it?'

'He was unlucky. We'll be all right if we all stick together,' Kenwyn said.

'How's that coupling coming along?' Kelly's voice asked over the intercom.

'We're all done here,' Anna said.

'Excellent,' Kelly said. I've got a few more jobs which need your attention.'

They spent an uncomfortable night camped in the Dining Room. Worried about the risks of aftershocks, they had agreed to stay together in the room nearest the airlock. They still wore their exosuits with their helmets close at hand, just in case the pressure dropped again. Unfortunately, like dinner, Wai and Tony had separated themselves from the rest of them and now whispered continually, which further annoyed Kelly. Afraid to further alienate them, she said nothing, her frustration rising and sleep not forthcoming.

At first light, they recommenced restoring the scattered items into their rightful places while Kenwyn prepared breakfast for the group. Once they had eaten, Tony and the medic ventured outside.

'Look at that,' the assistant commander said. 'The radiation shield's worked loose and torn right through the inflatable part of the structure.'

'That must have been some force. That panel is several inches thick, and it's buckled.'

'Well, it's totally useless now,' Tony said flatly. 'To make matters worse, it's my room that's open to the elements.'

'I'm sorry about that,' Kenwyn said, pulling the parts of the torn inflatable together in an attempt to see if it was repairable. 'If I set about mending the inner, can you fabricate a replacement panel?'

'Of course. Give us a hand to take down this broken section, and then I can use it as a template.'

161

The two men worked hard to remove the hanging metal sheet before it finally clanged to the ground. Once the defective panel had been removed, the true extent of the damage to the internal structure became apparent.

'That's going to take some fixing,' Tony said, surveying the tear. 'We'll need one of the others to help repair this from the inside.'

Kenwyn flicked the switch on his helmet's intercom.

'Anna, can you suit up and lend a helping hand.'

'Yep, give me a few seconds,' her voice crackling in his ears.

'Once you are suited, can you ask Kelly to let you into the sleeping quarters? I'm going to need your help fixing the inner lining.'

'Roger that.'

Dressed in her exosuit and helmet, Anna stood by the door, which led to the decompressed section of the structure. Anything not fixed down had since been removed or hidden in drawers and cupboards, so they would not have to tidy the Dining Room again.

'Are you ready?' Kelly asked over the intercom from behind the closed door of the Ops Room.

Anna gave her a thumbs-up through the glass.

'Hold onto something,' Kelly said. 'The blast of air might knock you over.'

The Russian engineer wrapped her right arm through the grab rail next to the steel door. Using an access code which only she and Tony knew, Kelly released the lock. Anna pulled open the door, releasing a loud hiss as the pressure equalized between the two compartments, pinning her to the wall. It took her a few moments to find her footing then she disappeared down the corridor. Kelly secured the door remotely, and re-pressurized the Dining Room.

The sleeping quarters were a mess. The earthquake and the sudden pressure drop had disturbed most of their personal belongings which now littered the floor. The sight of her things strewn around the room saddened Anna. The force of the decompression had even opened drawers, scattering items indiscriminately. Even the porcelain ballerina her father had given her for her eighteenth birthday now lay in pieces. She knelt down, holding the largest fragments in her gloved hands, her eyes welling up.

Moving from room to room, she inspected the walls for signs of structural damage. Most of the sleeping quarters lay in a similar state of disarray to hers, with only Kelly's, at the end of the corridor, remaining undisturbed. As she entered Tony's room, Kenwyn's face greeted her from outside.

'I wish you'd use the airlock like everyone else,' she laughed.

'You know me. I always do the unexpected. Tony and I can only find this area of damage.'

'The other rooms look okay. What do you think caused it? I thought the dome was meant to be earthquake-proof.'

'Somehow, one of the radiation shields buckled and it tore through the internal lining as it worked loose.

'Bummer.'

'Can you clear some space in there? Push all that

stuff to one side, so you can work freely.'

Anna swept Tony's things towards the wall, creating sufficient room for her to stand comfortably. Kenwyn started handing her tools through the giant hole as the two of them began sealing the tear in the inner structure.

Apart from their mandatory radiation breaks, they worked solidly for several hours, fixing and mending.

'Well done,' Anna said into her microphone as the medic placed the last patch over the damaged inflatable, hiding his face.

'I just hope it holds. Anyway, we'd better go back inside before the temperature drops,' the medic commented.

'It's already getting cold,' she said, checking the gauge on her left wrist. 'Do you think we can re-pressurize this part tonight?'

'Probably. But we won't be able to move in until tomorrow; the radiation shield won't be ready.'

'So, it's another night in the Dining Room, then?'

'Sure is.'

The rumble of the airlock signaled Kenwyn's return.

'Let's start re-pressurizing,' he said into the dome's intercom.

'Okay, but stay there,' Kelly instructed, locked in the Ops Room with Tony and Wai. 'I just need to let Anna in.'

A series of clunks resonated through the structure as the internal door unlocked, followed by a loud hiss as Anna opened the internal, steel door. Kelly re-pressurized the front half of the dome while Anna, still wearing her exosuit and helmet, sat on one of the tables with her feet resting on one of the benches.

'It's okay, Kelly announced after an hour, opening the door. 'The pressure's back to normal.'

Anna removed her helmet as Kenwyn joined them from the airlock and the rest of the crew emerged from the safety of the Ops Room.

'Wai, the door between the corridor and the greenhouse remained locked. Through the glass, everything looks fine.'

'Thank God,' the botanist said. 'If that had decompressed all my work so far would have been for nothing.'

'Where was the breach?' Kelly asked.

'Tony's room,' Anna said. 'I'm sorry, but it looks like a war zone after the rapid decompression.'

'Great,' he replied sarcastically. 'What else can go wrong?'

'How did you get on with preparing the replacement panel?' Kenwyn asked, trying to change the subject.

'It's in the kiln,' Tony answered dismissively. 'We should be able to install it tomorrow.'

'Great. As soon as it's in place, we can re-pressurize the whole dome. Then we can move back into our quarters.'

'So, we're spending another night cramped in here?' Wai asked exasperatedly.

'It's only one more night,' Kelly said. 'Once the integrity of the outer structure has been restored, everything will be as good as new.'

'It's not your room which has been destroyed,'

Tony hissed back angrily.

'Tony!' the commander scolded. 'I was only trying to say, considering how long it's taken us to get here, one extra night isn't going to make a difference.'

'I don't know what I can do!' Kelly said animatedly, reclining on an examination couch in the Infirmary. 'Whatever I say seems to be wrong.'

'It's all so unnecessary,' Kenwyn, commented, putting down his needle holders.

The medic dabbed the sutured wound with a gauze swab soaked in antiseptic, wiping away the trickle of blood which dribbled down the side of her face.

'Finished. I've tried my best, but I suspect it's going to leave a small scar.'

'That's the least of my worries,' she said, removing the sterile drape that was over her shirt.

She admired his handiwork in the mirror on the wall; the wound edges had been brought together neatly by three tiny, blue sutures.

'It looks very neat,' she said.

'You sound surprised,' he smiled. 'Keep it dry for twenty-four hours. I won't put anything on it, so the air gets to it, but you'll probably want to use one of these dressings if you're wearing your helmet. Otherwise, it will rub, and we might need to suture it again.

'Thanks,' she said, pocketing the handful of dressings he had given her. 'You don't think I'm over-reacting about Tony, do you?'

'No, he vehemently believes he should be the commander of this mission.'

'Well, he said as much, didn't he?'

166

'It wasn't really said, more like shouted,' he sniggered.

There was a knock on the door, causing the two of them to fall quiet.

'I've been looking for you,' Tony said, staring straight at Kenwyn and ignoring Kelly. 'The replacement radiation shield is out of the kiln. It'll be ready in the morning once it's had a chance to cool.'

'Thanks. Then we can return to sleeping in our own beds. The good news is the pressure in the dome is holding, so the repairs have worked.'

Tony nodded and began to leave.

'By the way,' he said over his shoulder. 'If you're going to talk about me, try and make it less obvious.'

The door slammed as he left, prompting Kelly to roll her eyes before muttering something unrepeatable under her breath.

23.

'The new panel's secured in position,' Tony said into his helmet microphone as he and Kenwyn stood back to study their handiwork.

'Roger that. Thanks, you two. 'Kelly said into the intercom mounted on the wall. 'Anna, what's the Geiger counter readings like in there?'

'It's too early to tell', the Russian engineer said, looking up from her tablet. 'We should leave it for an hour then check the levels.'

'Okay,' the commander said. 'Everyone, you heard her, the corridor stays locked for the time being.'

There were groans from the rest of the crew.

To boost morale, Kelly made coffee for all the team as the two men returned inside. Out of habit, she filled a cup for Mac but quickly poured it away before anyone noticed. An uncomfortable silence hung over them as they waited for the sleeping quarters to re-pressurize. Surprisingly, Tony sat opposite her, though he did not speak or make eye contact.

'What's the deal with the accommodation block?' Anna asked. 'Does it need to be finished before the Discovery lands?'

'We must complete the ground floor before they arrive,' Kelly said. 'Otherwise, they'll have to stay on the ship until the construction's completed. The other level can wait until we have extra hands around to help with the build.'

'Most of the external panels are finished,' Kenwyn said. 'Tony and I could make a start on the building later today.'

'That would be excellent. Tony, are you up to it?' Kelly asked.

'Of course, I am,' he snapped back.

'Great,' she said, ignoring his annoyance.

Anna checked the computer screen, 'Your hour's up,' she chirped. 'And the levels in the corridor are back to normal.'

Without another word, everyone stood up, scraping their chairs on the floor.

Her room was located at the opposite end of the corridor from Tony's. Luckily, only a couple of her items had been disturbed. Most notably, the screen on the wall above her desk now hung at a jaunty angle. It did not take her long to restore her belongings to their rightful places before lying down on her bed. Emotion overwhelmed her, and she began sobbing uncontrollably into her pillow. Not having seen Ryan for many months, Mac's death and all the issues with Tony had made her emotional. All she wanted was a big hug.

Drying her eyes, she tried hailing her husband

aboard the Discovery. After a few minutes, his face appeared on the screen in front of her.

'Hey! How are you doing?' he asked, his smiling face instantly bringing comfort.

'Not good.'

'Why, what's up?'

She explained how her relationship with Tony had deteriorated further, and the awful tension which now existed inside the dome. Ryan said nothing, sitting and listening, as he had done many times before over the years. He never interrupted her, just letting her talk.

'How are you going to resolve it?' he asked eventually.

'I'm not sure. I was hoping things would blow over.'

'I suspect it's gone too far for that.'

'Whenever I speak to him, he bites my head off,' she said. 'I'm really unsure what to do. Anyway, enough of my moaning, what's happening up there on the Discovery?'

'We're still waiting for one of the colonists to die.'

'How awful.'

'The medics say there's no hope for her.'

'What about the others?'

'Everyone else is on the mend. Apparently, we can touch down as soon as the sick colonist has died, and we've jettisoned the body. The Agency say we're safe to land, providing no one else gets ill in the meantime.'

Suddenly, angry shouting emanated from outside her room.

'What's that noise?' asked Ryan.

'Not sure. It sounds like Tony's having a

meltdown. I'm going to have to call you back,' she cancelled the call causing the screen to go black.

In the corridor, Tony stood, ranting while Kenwyn tried to pacify him.

'Do you have it?' he screamed venomously on seeing Kelly.

'Do I have what?' she asked, having never seeing Tony this angry before. 'What's this about?

'Look at her? As if butter wouldn't melt in her mouth. You know full well what I mean.'

'Tony, calm down. I can assure you.....'

'Don't you tell me to calm down! If you and your cronies had not gone rifling through my belongings, I would be calm.'

Anna opened the giant steel door from the Dining Room to see what all the noise was about.

'What are you talking about?' the medic said, trying to remain composed. 'I'm sure no one has been going through your things?'

'If it wasn't her,' Tony shouted, looking hatefully at Kelly. 'Then, she's made one of you two do it for her.'

'Do you mean Anna and me?' the medic asked. 'Anna only went into your room to repair the dome's lining.'

'So, you admit you went into my room, then?' Tony bellowed, now red in the face.

'You know she did. How else would we have repaired the tear in the dome?'

'Well, it gave you plenty of time to steal my coin,' he continued, saliva spraying wildly from his mouth.

'Which coin?' Anna asked, somewhat perplexed.

'You know which coin,' he stammered, pounding his fist onto the steel wall. 'It's a silver dollar. My great-grandfather carried it with him through the

Second World War.'

'Tony, I can honestly say I didn't see any coins when I was in your room,' Anna said.

'Well, it's not. there now.'

Wai appeared, hearing the commotion. She looked at Kenwyn and Kelly with disappointment in her eyes before leading the assistant commander towards the greenhouse.

'What the hell was that about?' Anna asked, visibly shaken.

'Something to do with some coin or something,' the medic said.

'I saw him kiss it before we launched and again before landing,' Kelly said, losing her temper. 'The damn thing must have gone missing when the dome depressurized.'

'Where does he get off talking to us like that, though?' asked Anna.

'I guess he's having trouble adjusting to being here,' Kelly said. 'Especially with his illness and everything.'

'Doesn't he realize it's been tough for all of us,' the engineer said. 'It doesn't excuse his behavior.'

'Cut him some slack,' said Kelly. 'We've all been through a lot.'

That evening, Kelly, Kenwyn and Anna cooked dinner. Despite everything, there was a light-hearted feeling among them while they prepared a meal which had been missing for some time.

'When do you think the Discovery will land?' the medic asked, ladling out food onto the trays in front of him.'

'Any day now,' Kelly replied. 'It's a grim business, though. What must it be like, waiting for someone to die, knowing your mission is on hold until they do.'

'Dinner's ready,' Anna called into the intercom for the others.

'I can't imagine what it must be like,' she said. 'Are we going to be safe when they land?'

'Yes, I've checked. We've all been vaccinated against it,' the medic said.

'That's good news,' said Kelly, sitting down at the table with her tray. 'How can you be sure the vaccines have worked?'

'The hantavirus vaccine usually has a high success rate,' he said. 'But I can test everybody's antibodies levels to make sure.'

'In the circumstances, it's probably the right thing to do,' Kelly said. 'We don't need an outbreak down here.'

'What do we have to watch out for,' Anna asked uncomfortably. 'You know, just in case.'

'Hantavirus can be easy to overlook,' Kenwyn explained. 'Because the first features are similar to influenza.'

'So, fever, headache and muscles aches then?' asked Anna.

'Yes,' said Kenwyn. 'So, you think you've had the flu and think no more of it. In a small number of patients, about a week after the initial illness settle, they develop a severe cough and shortness of breath. In the last significant outbreak on Earth, roughly forty percent of people who caught it died.'

'How many people have been infected on the Discovery?'

'Most of the colonists, but the death rate has been

considerably lower than that,' said Kelly.

'I would be happier if I knew the vaccine had worked,' Anna said, reaching across the table for a piece of bread.

'I'll test everyone's titers tomorrow,' he said.

The steel door creaked open, causing everyone to look up. Wai entered cautiously before closing it behind her.

'Wai,' Kelly said. 'Come and join us.'

'Okay,' she said nervously, removing a tray from the rack on the wall.

'We were talking about the arrival of the new colonists,' Kelly said. 'It should be any day now.'

'To be honest, I'm looking forward to it,' Wai said, spooning food onto her tray. 'All those people arriving might dilute the tension in this place.'

'I hope so,' said Kelly gently.

'I'm going to need a blood sample from you and Tony tomorrow to make sure your antibody levels are high enough to cover you against the infection on the Discovery,' Kenwyn said.

The expression on Wai's face dropped, 'I hate needles,' she mumbled.

'I'm the same,' Anna said. 'but then I'm not sure any of us enjoy them.'

'I suppose you're right', she said, taking a mouthful of food.

'Will Tony be joining us for dinner?' the medic asked, standing up and transferring his dirty tray to the washer.

'No,' she said glumly. 'I don't think so.'

'He's very welcome to join us,' Kelly said. 'It would be nice for us to sit down as a group again before the colonists arrive.'

'I don't think he will, he's too angry.'

They finished eating in silence before Wai stood up, taking another tray from the rack.

'I'd better take some for him,' she said.

'Of course,' the medic said. 'Are you not staying for dessert?'

'No, I should really take this back to him.'

She plated out some of the remaining food and disappeared through the steel door towards the sleeping quarters.

'This is becoming intolerable,' Kelly whispered once the heavy door had closed.

'It's awful, isn't it?' said the medic. 'Now, he won't even sit in the same room as us.'

'I feel sorry for Wai,' Anna added. 'She seems to be stuck in the middle.'

'How do we resolve this?' asked Kelly. 'I'm out of ideas, and things keep getting worse.'

24.

The remaining sick colonist onboard the Discovery refused to die while the prolonged isolation of the remaining crew of the Aeolis had led to a catastrophic deterioration in relations. Inside the dome was almost as toxic as the Martian atmosphere. The two factions now barely spoke. When they did, only sharp, terse words were exchanged, further adding fuel to the fire. Battlelines had been drawn. Tony spent all his time with Wai, the two of them rarely interacting with the rest of the crew. They inhabited the last two rooms on the corridor, preferring to spend most of their time in the greenhouse. Kelly and the others occupied the Ops Room. Out of necessity, the Dining Room, the airlock and the bathrooms were deemed neutral territory, but the two groups avoided each other unless absolutely necessary. Tony and Wai would not go onto the surface together, afraid someone would disable the airlock, preventing them from getting back in. Similarly, Kelly and her allies took it in turn to remain in the dome.

Despite the enmity which now existed, the construction proceeded at pace. The increasing number of buildings on the crater floor formed a semi-circle, facing the landing zone. The dome's support systems, the environmental control and waste re-cycling units, now supplied all the structures in their small community. In addition, newly-dug access tunnels, which they called 'umbilicals,' now ran between the different buildings, reducing the need to go outside. The narrow, machine-carved tubes had been lined by Tony's mars-rock panels, improving the aesthetics while simultaneously supporting the roof, but still, these cramped, claustrophobic spaces terrified Anna. Not quite high enough to walk through, she shuffled on her hands and knees, routing cables from the turbines back towards the dome, frequently banging her head on the low ceiling.

Even with the ongoing feud, Tony continued to manufacture the materials needed for the developing colony, but did so on his own, without talking with the others. Kenwyn would write the next day's requirements on the whiteboard, and the assistant commander completed the order.

Emerging from the tunnel into the taller ladder room, Anna brushed herself down then set about connecting the power lines to a junction box. It took her an hour to feed the wires inside the giant, green casing and securing them to the correct terminals.

'Right, Kelly,' she said into the intercom mounted on the wall. 'Try it.'

'Roger,' the scratchy voice acknowledged.

'We have power,' the voice returned after a few seconds. 'Good job.'

'I'm off to have a well-deserved cuppa.'

'You do that. Once you've finished your break, can you give Kenwyn a hand outside'?

'Will do,'

Kelly walked from room to room, inspecting the quality of the construction of the ground floor of the accommodation block. She was proud of their achievements, considering the circumstances. Through the airlock, which was not yet operational, Kelly watched Anna join Kenwyn on the surface. Despite their exosuits and helmets, she could tell from their body language, they were more than just crewmates. She envied them, missing having somebody to hug and being able to talk in confidence to someone who understood her. Feeling down, she stared thoughtfully into the distance. The daylight began to disappear over the distant hills, turning the sky a mixture of scarlet and mauve when something caught her eye, glinting through the plexiglass in the evening sun.

'I wonder,' she muttered to herself.

She hurried along the umbilical then ascended the ladder, coming out in the dome's Generator Room. Despite knowing the rules about all of them being outside, it would only be for a brief moment. After slipping on her exosuit and donning her helmet, Kelly tapped the code into the keypad then lowered the lever.

It had been some time since she had ventured beyond the walls of the dome, and the appearance of the fledgling colony had changed considerably. Making her way towards the accommodation block, she tried to locate the object which had been reflecting the sun's rays. Whatever it was, it continued to cast shimmering patterns onto the window. Bending down, Kelly ran her fingers over the dusty ground and, as she suspected, found a silver dollar. Presumably, it was the one Tony had lost. She could think of no other reason why there would be any others on Mars. It must have been sucked outside by the rapid decompression during the earthquake. She secured the coin in the front pocket of her exosuit before heading back inside. Hopefully, returning it to Tony would help alleviate some of the tension which existed between them.

Happy with herself, Kelly proceeded back through the airlock, removed her helmet and suit as soon as the light changed color. Dressed in her t-shirt and shorts, the only things which fitted comfortably under the snug exosuit, she ripped off the claustrophobic thyroid shield then hung up her suit on the rack of hangers. Unzipping the pocket, Kelly retrieved the coin then stared out through the window at the last rays of sunshine. Behind her, someone entered the room from inside the dome. She turned to see whether it was Tony or Wai when something struck her across the back of the head. There was a fleeting flash of light before everything went dark as the silver dollar fell to the floor.

***

Waking up in unfamiliar surroundings is disconcerting. His head hurt, and there was an overwhelming sense of nausea. Something choked him, making swallowing extremely difficult. His eyes darted around the room. Wherever he was, it appeared familiar, but at the same time, it all looked wrong. He tried to sit up, but there were restraints around his wrists and ankles. Panicked, he fought against them, attempting to shout for help.

Desperately turning his head from side to side, his eyes searched the surroundings, but he could not move sufficiently to locate a door. Trying to regain control of his emotions, he took stock of the situation, but his overactive brain swirled with fear and confusion. A metal door opened, out of his field of view, followed by footsteps on the checker-plate floor.

'It's okay,' a man's voice came from behind him. 'You're safe now.'

Mac attempted to speak, but whatever was in his mouth prevented him.

'Relax,' said the emotionless voice. 'I'll take that out.'

He felt some movement at his shoulder before having the unpleasant experience of a tube being pulled up through his larynx, prompting him to let out a harsh, wet cough.

'It will stop irritating soon.'

'Where am I?' Mac croaked, somewhat confused.

'Don't worry. You're okay now,

'My crewmates will be looking for me,' he said, his voice pleading. 'I have to get back to them.'

'I'm sorry, but no one is looking for you.'

What's your name?' the Scotsman asked, trying to

befriend his captor.

'My name is Peter. I rescued you.'

'Are you one of the new colonists?'

'No,' the voice said calmly. 'I'm not a colonist. Now rest a while. You must be exhausted. This will help you.'

A sinister-looking gloved hand placed an oxygen mask over Mac's mouth, and nose before the door behind him closed again with a metallic thud followed by the unmistakable sound of bolts being drawn into place. Mac tried to sit up but was restricted by the restraints. Fighting against them, he struggled to get free, but they did not yield.

He could feel his pulse pounding in his ears as he looked around the room. Hanging from a dripstand next to the bed, a colorless, plastic tube connected a bag of fluid to an intravenous cannula in his left forearm. The rest of the room looked similar to the Medical Bay on the Aeolis, but it was bigger and a subtly different color. Beside him, a syringe driver whirred to life as it pumped drugs into him, which caused him to sleep again.

Mac drifted in and out of consciousness for several hours, struggling to distinguish his dreams from reality. Throughout all of it, the calm, yet unsettling, voice of Peter remained.

'Good morning, Michael,' he said. 'I hope you slept well.

Mac tried to sit up but was restricted by his restraints.

'Don't struggle,' he said, from out of his eyeline. 'I've brought you some breakfast.'

'Why am I restrained?' he asked angrily.

'You were a little combative when I rescued you. It's for your own safety.'

'I'm not combative now. Can you let me go?'

'All in good time. Now, you must be starving.'

From behind him, a food tray was placed in front of him. Mac noticed the stranger wore a leather glove. Craning his neck, he tried to see the elusive man who now haunted his dreams, but despite his best efforts, he could only catch a fleeting glimpse of a man wearing a black hood.

'I'm going to release your right hand so you can eat. Please don't struggle.'

Peter pressed a hidden button, and the restraint came loose. Mac stretched his aching wrist.

'Enjoy your breakfast,' Peter said emotionlessly before leaving.

Mac scanned the tray in, it contained a small quantity of scrambled eggs, a slice of toast and a plastic tumbler of water. He quickly shoveled the food into his mouth using his free hand, ignoring the fork which had been provided. Next, he turned his attention to his other wrist.

'Michael,' came the eerie voice over the intercom. 'Please do not interfere with the restraints.'

Mac froze. Peter was watching him.

'Let me out of here,' he shouted into the empty room. 'Why are you keeping me like this?'

'It's for your own safety,' the voice repeated, flat and monotonous.

'I demand you let me go,' he screamed.

'Michael, there's no need to get excited. Did you enjoy your breakfast?'

Mac did not answer.

'Why are you so ungrateful? You're lucky to be alive.'

'I'm extremely grateful, but let me go, please,' he begged.

'There is nowhere to go, Michael.'

'What do you mean?'

'I found you and saved your life. You would have died if I hadn't brought you here.'

'I don't understand.'

'You were stranded in your Rover a long way from home with virtually no oxygen.'

Peter pulled up a chair, sitting next to him. For the first time, Mac could see the person he had been talking to. Average height and build, wearing a jacket with an improvised hood which covered most of his face.

'Where are we?'

'You're on board the Erebus, or should I say, what's left of her.'

'How can that be? The Erebus was destroyed attempting to land. All the crew were killed.'

'That's not quite true. Three of us survived and parts of the ship are still habitable.'

'So where are the others?'

'Sadly, they succumbed to their injuries,' he said, demonstrating no emotion. 'I've been alone for some time.'

'I'm sorry to hear that,' Mac said, trying to appear sympathetic. 'Why haven't you communicated with Earth or our base in the Gusev Crater?'

'All communication systems were damaged beyond repair in the crash. Thankfully, the reactor works, and I still have enough supplies. So, I've had to eke out a lonely existence.'

183

'Why don't we go to the others at the dome? It'll be less isolated.'

'All in good time,' he said dismissively.

Peter resecured Mac's free hand in the restraint and left, taking the tray with him.

25.

Kelly felt herself being pulled along the corridor like a rag doll. Her head lolled from side to side while her feet dragged uncontrollably behind her. Forced onto a chair in the corner of a cramped room, her wrists and ankles were secured crudely and masking tape was applied over her mouth, muffling her whimpers. She never caught site of her assailant, but it had to be Tony.

Her head hung forward, battered and defeated. A mixture of blood and sweat dripped from her left cheek, collecting in a small pool on the floor. Sobbing uncontrollably, her eyes darted around the dark space.

The heavy air tasted musty and fetid; leaving a residual, metallic taste lingering on her tongue. Darkness surrounded her, the only light coming from under the door. She leant back in the chair, unsure where she was. An unusual humming noise droned continually accompanied by the faint sound of dripping water. With only one way in and no windows, wherever this was, she knew the others would never find her. How had it come to this?

***

Tony crept down the corridor, listening to the tone of the voices emanating from the Dining Room. One by one, he checked the bedrooms for any of the other crew members. Thankfully, they were empty. Without hesitating, he tapped in a code on the control panel, locking the metal door before scurrying away. No one could rescue her now.

Kenwyn was cleaning dust from his boots when the door locked. Through the glass, he caught sight of the assistant commander disappearing into the greenhouse. He tried the door, but it was fastened shut.

'Tony!' he bellowed, slamming his fist repeatedly on the bulkhead. 'Open this door. Tony!'

No reply.

He pressed the buttons on the dome's intercom, 'All crew members to the Dining Room immediately.'

'What is it?' Anna asked, her face inquisitive as she poked her head out of the Generator Room.

'Where's Kelly?' he barked desperately.

'I'm not sure. Last time I saw her, she was outside.'

'Have you seen Wai?'

'Not for a while.'

He ran to the airlock, beginning to count the exosuits out loud.

'Damn. There are five.'

'Kenwyn, what's going on? You're not making any sense.'

'Tony's locked the door between the Dining Room and the sleeping quarters. Only he and Kelly have the key and her suit is here, meaning he's got her in there.'

'Perhaps she's in the accommodation block.'

'She would have been here by now,' he snapped at her, his frustration bubbling over.

'You don't think they've kidnapped her, do you?'

'Why else would he lock the door?'

The two of them searched the dome and surrounding buildings, looking in every room they had access to. Every storage room and cupboard was opened, but there was no trace of the commander.

'He's taken her.' Kenwyn growled.

'What should we do?'

'I don't know.'

'One of us should suit up and walk around to the greenhouse,' Anna suggested.

'How will that help?'

'At least we'd be certain they have her.'

'Where else do you think she's going to be?' he snapped.

'Surely, he wouldn't hurt her,' she said. 'He's not that stupid.'

'Who knows?'

They sat speechlessly in the Dining Room, absorbing the magnitude of the situation.

'You need to call the Discovery and tell Ryan,' Anna said finally.

'That's not going to be an easy conversation.'

'But at least you know him,' she said. 'I haven't met him. If I called him, it might make things even worse.'

They moved through to the Operations Room,

Kenwyn rehearsing what he would say as Anna closed the door behind him. Nothing seemed adequate or appropriate. Whichever combination of words he used; it was going to sound bad. Nonetheless, he eventually plucked up the courage and typed the number into the keyboard on the desk. An intermittent tone rang from the speakers before the call was answered. Ryan's face appeared on the large screen; the busy deck of his ship visible behind him.

'Where's Kelly?' he asked, clearly surprised by Kenwyn's face.

'We have a problem,' the medic said reluctantly.

'Go on,' said Ryan.

'We think there's been a mutiny and Kelly may have been kidnapped by Tony Zaragosi.'

'This is some kind of joke, right?'

'I wish it was,' Kenwyn said, his usual smile absent. 'We've been locked out of part of the dome and Kelly's missing. Their relationship has broken down over the last few months.'

'She told me things were getting bad. I should have listened more,' Ryan said, visibly distressed. 'I should contact the Agency and take their guidance on how to proceed. Does he have any weapons?'

'Firearms were not allowed onboard the Aeolis, but he will have access to gardening implements, knives and stuff.'

'Okay. Is Tony acting alone?'

'We think Wai Xu may be involved. They have sealed themselves into the greenhouses and sleeping quarters.'

'Do they have food and water?' he asked, his mind racing.

'They do have water, it is supplied directly to the

greenhouse's irrigation system, but they won't have anything to eat, only the plants which are growing.'

'Okay, in a strange way, that's good. It won't force them into doing anything stupid. '

'Should I turn off the water supply,' Anna asked. 'It might bring this situation to a quick end.'

'No,' said Ryan. 'Don't irritate them. They're angry enough already, I don't want to make things worse for Kelly. I'll speak to the Agency. We'll try and resolve this as quickly and as peacefully as we can. Keep yourselves safe. Avoid speaking to them if you can, we don't want to aggravate things. I'll be back in touch as soon as I hear back from the Agency.'

'How long do you think it'll take?' Kenwyn asked.

'Anything up to twenty-five minutes,' he said. 'I'll contact you when I have instructions, but it won't be quick.'

'Okay,' said the medic. 'If anything changes, can I call you?'

'Of course.'

The screen went black.

Kenwyn slumped back in the chair, 'This is horrible.'

'I can't sit here and not doing anything. I'm going to walk around the outside of the dome and see if they're in the greenhouse,' Anna said.

'No. You heard Ryan, don't antagonize them. You know how tightly wound Tony is right now.'

'I won't.'

***

'It's good you rest,' Peter said with his usual emotional detachment.

Mac wriggled, gradually opening his eyes.

'There is not much else to do here,' he replied, rattling his restraints.

'I don't sleep,' said Peter, adjusting his hood nervously to cover his face. 'I only steal a few minutes every now and then.'

'What's the problem?'

'I relive the crash,' his voice faltering. 'Every night, without fail.'

'Why don't you tell me about it. You might find it helps.'

'You'll have to bear with me, it's very hard to discuss.'

'I understand.'

'We were on final approach, heading towards our landing site on the Hellas plains when we hit an uncharted mountain.'

'How awful.'

'Everyone was a little shaken, but the damage wasn't that bad. It was still flyable, so the pilot took manual control.'

'So, what happened?'

'We tried to gain altitude, preparing to land again, but the Erebus had a fundamental design flaw. At eight thousand feet, the ship started climbing erratically. At first, we thought it was due to the impact, but the instruments seemed to be working fine.'

'Go on,' said Mac, sensing Peter's emotions welling up.

'The wings on the Erebus were mounted quite far back on the fuselage, further back than on any previous space vehicle.'

'So, the weight of the engines made the front of the spacecraft to rise?' Mac suggested.

'Yes. The designers programmed the flight control systems to automatically correct for this by continuing to drop the front of the craft subtly during flight. The Agency didn't think it was important enough to tell us,' his voice getting angry for the first time. 'They expected the ship's systems to make small corrections to account for their design error without anyone being aware of it.'

'So, the crew were fighting against the computer?'

'Yes, it was futile. As we continued to climb, the computers thought the nose was rising, forcing the Erebus into a steep dive which no one could have pulled out of.'

'Sounds terrible. How did you survive?'

'I've said enough,' Peter stood up, self-consciously adjusting his hood again. 'I have to go.'

26.

Locked out of their quarters, they spent an uncomfortable night on the floor of the Dining Room. Kenwyn was first to wake and rose to his feet gingerly, trying not to disturb Anna. Out of desperation, he attempted to open the door again, but, predictably, it remained secure.

As he entered the airlock, his overwhelming emotional exhaustion and the cold air against his skin made him shiver. The dusty plateau outside was still shrouded in darkness, the sun only just beginning to illuminate the landscape. In the peculiar half-life, the numerous extinct, volcanoes on the horizon appeared black and foreboding. Kenwyn stood there for more than an hour as the sky turned from pink to its usual butterscotch-yellow color. As impressive as the rugged geography of Mars was, he missed living under blue skies. The Martian atmosphere felt ominous; sickly, curious even, but unsettling. It did not feel like home, serving as a warning for how dangerous this planet really was.

He walked back, tip-toeing past Anna, who still slept, making himself a cup of coffee in the small kitchen. Sitting on a cold bench behind one of the tables, he sipped tentatively, unsure what to do next. Should he carry on preparing for the Discovery's arrival, or try and resolve their current issue? He wished Kelly was here.

A high-pitched ping brought him back from his thoughts- an incoming message. Hurrying over Anna, he jogged to the Ops Room. Leaning across the desk, he pressed the keyboard. The screen illuminated, bringing Ryan's face into focus.

'Morning, Kenwyn. Any news?'

'Nothing, we've been locked in the Dining Room all night.'

'Well, our last Hantavirus patient has just died; everyone else is still asymptomatic. The Agency are fully aware of the situation down there, but they don't want to risk the virus getting into the Mars ecosystem. They've advised us to stay in orbit until our quarantine period is over. So, we can come down to the surface in forty-eight hours, providing no one develops any new symptoms.'

'Okay,' the medic replied, finding it hard to hide his disappointment.

'Any sign of Kelly?'

'No. We've not had any contact with them since the door was locked.'

'I'll bring a security team with me, but hopefully, it won't come to that.'

'I hope not.'

'If anything changes, call me. Bye.'

The screen went blank.

'How have we ended up with armed guards

coming to our home,' Anna said, sitting on the floor, propped against the wall.

'I know, it feels as if we've failed, even more than if we hadn't found water.'

'I'm worried how this will play out. We're a long way from the group of friends who stood on that stage back at the Agency.'

'I hoped turning off the water would bring this to a swift conclusion, but it's made little difference.'

'Wai has large storage units in the plant nursery. They're probably using those. It might be weeks before they run out.'

***

She had needed the bathroom during the long night, but having been abandoned, tied to the chair. An hour ago, she had had no other option but to soil herself. Ashamed and alone, she sobbed uncontrollably.

The door crashed open, in marched Tony, his eyes fervid and wild.

'I'm going to make you pay for the way you've humiliated me,' he snarled.

Gagged and restrained, she stared at him, wide-eyed, her pupils dilated. Something moved in her peripheral vision. Wai stood awkwardly from the safety of the greenhouse, silhouetted by the early morning sun behind her. Tony pulled a combat knife from his belt, waving it intimidatingly in front of Kelly. Recoiling, she let out a muffled cry as the blade swished inches from her nose. He laughed menacingly, re-sheathing it before leaving the room.

Once he had gone, the botanist rushed in, carrying some item in her arms.

'This is going to hurt,' she said gently, pulling the tape off.

'Thank you,' Kelly said, relieved the adhesive was gone.

Wai opened a bottle of water and held it to Kelly's lips. Spilling more than she swallowed, she drank greedily, appreciating the opportunity to rinse out her mouth.

'What's going on? Why's this happening?'

'It's Tony,' Wai said, pouring some antiseptic into a receptacle. 'He believes you have betrayed him.'

'Betrayed him, how?' she asked, wincing as the solution made contact with her grazed face.

'He feels you constantly undermined him.'

'I haven't done anything of the sort,' she said, racking her brains for anything which could have precipitated this.

'You made Kenwyn, your deputy without telling him. Tony's a very proud man.'

'Only while Tony was ill,' she tried to explain. 'As soon as he was fit again, I was going to restore him to his post.'

'He's not going to believe that.'

'He thinks Mac would be alive if it wasn't for you. He holds you solely responsible for his death.'

'That's crazy. What was I supposed to do? Lead more of the crew to their deaths in search of a corpse.'

'He has a different perspective.'

'Wai, let me go,' Kelly pleaded. 'It doesn't have to be like this.'

'I can't. Tony would be angry,' she whispered, replacing the tape back over Kelly's mouth.

27.

The room appeared smaller in the Erebus' dim, night time lighting. Having slept fitfully, Mac was unsure of the time. Lying in a similar position for several days had taken its toll on his aching body. His lower back, elbows and heels throbbed. He attempted to get more comfortable, pulling up against his restraints. The left one was looser than usual. He repeatedly flexed and extended his biceps, applying stress to it. Gradually, the encircling cuff weakened, the screw holding it in place loosening. Just as he was about to free his hand, the lights changed - now it was daytime. He froze. Peter was now likely to be awake and probably watching, so Mac laid back on the bed, pretending not to be awake.

Presently, Peter arrived with a breakfast tray. The quality of the food had deteriorated even since Mac had first been aboard the Erebus. Having a visitor was clearly putting a strain on Peter's supplies.

'Thank you,' he said, as the hooded man unfastened Mac's right hand and ankles, allowing him to eat.

'How are you feeling today?' Peter asked. 'Good, I hope.'

'I slept well, thanks,' he lied.

Mac probed the contents of the plate with the fork, unimpressed by the meagre offering.

'I've been wondering,' Mac said. 'How did you find me in the storm?'

'Pure luck, if I'm honest. It caught me by surprise too,' he replied. 'The visibility was horrendous, and I couldn't see a thing as I headed back towards the Erebus. Out of the gloom your Rover appeared in front of me. I almost crashed into you. You were in a bad way when I found you. If I had arrived a couple of minutes later, I don't think you would have made it.'

'I'm glad you did, but how did you find your way back?'

'Storms are common here. I've got used to driving when it's bad. I brought you back in your Rover here, then went back for mine on foot when it had all calmed down.'

'Well, I'm really grateful.' Mac said. 'What happened to the rest of your crew?'

'I understand you're curious, but I'd rather not talk about it.'

'Were you injured?' he persisted.

'Yes, I will always bear the scars of that day,' he said. 'Physically and emotionally.'

'You have done well to survive this long on your own. I'm not sure I could have. How long is it now?'

'Two years and four months.'

'Ah! Yes. Erebus used the launch window before ours.'

'That's right.'

'Last night, it dawned on me,' said Mac, finishing the food. 'You must be Dr Peter McCarthy, the Erebus' medic.'

'I am indeed, and you are Michael McDonald. We met once before at the Agency.'

'Yes, I remember now. It was at some fundraising dinner. I forget what for.'

'Shall I take these away?' Peter asked, reaching out with his gloved hand.

'Thank you. I'm afraid I need the bathroom.'

'Don't worry. Let me clear these things away then I'll be back.'

Alone in the room, Mac worked feverishly to break the restraint on his left hand. Wrenching it back and forth, it eventually fell apart. He reassembled it around his wrist, giving the impression it was still intact as Peter returned, wheeling a commode. The mysterious medic erected a screen to preserve Mac's modesty before leaving the room again. Stretching his legs, Mac snuck out, positioning himself to the side of the door, out of sight of the cameras.

He waited for several minutes before shouting, 'I've finished,' he hollered.

A few moments later, the door slid open. As Peter stepped into the room, Mac punched his unsuspecting captor squarely in the abdomen. The hooded figure doubled over; his head forcibly meeting Mac's knee. The shorter man fell backwards into the corridor, letting out a howl, the hood falling from his head. The sight which greeted Mac disgusted him. The right side of the man's face was melted like candle wax, his lips frozen in a contorted grimace where the scar tissue had contracted over time. Most of Peter's hair was missing, his right eye closed and distorted.

'This is how you repay me,' the scarred man yelled.

'You were keeping me captive,' Mac shouted back.

'I saved your life!' the man said desperately, quickly pulling his hood back over his face. 'I wanted us to be friends.'

'Friends?' Mac asked in disbelief, his voice raised. 'Friend don't keep each other restrained like pets.'

'I told you,' Peter replied angrily. 'You were combative.'

'Only when I first arrived,' Mac ranted. 'I couldn't breathe.'

'I couldn't let you see me looking like this,' he mumbled finally.

Mac stopped himself from shouting back, fighting the anger that burned inside of him. This man was clearly struggling with the events and isolation of the past two years. What unimaginable horrors had he experienced? Mac took a deep breath and held out his hand, helping Peter to his feet.

**

His eyes were wilder than before. Tony strode up to her, kicked the chair before ripping the tape from her mouth.

'Right, you bitch, I'm going to make you pay for what you've done.'

'Tony, whatever I've done to offend you, I'm sorry,' she said. 'Can we talk about it?'

'Don't you try and trick me with your words. You

have constantly undermined me since we arrived.'

'When did I undermine you?'

'You made your pet, Kenwyn, assistant commander.' He spat the medic's name at her.

'You were ill. I needed Kenwyn to step up while you were incapacitated.'

'Oh! So, it's my fault. Look at what you're doing, you're twisting everything to manipulate those around you, just like you always do.'

'What do you mean?'

'You turned everyone against me with your constant drip-feed of toxic comments.'

'I've done no such thing. My whole crew are important to me, you included.'

'Then, how do you explain this?' he said defiantly as he produced the coin from his pocket. 'You had it in your hand in the airlock.'

'I found it outside after the earthquake.'

'A likely story.'

'What possible reason could I have for stealing it?'

'To undermine me!'

'Come on, Tony. Be rational.'

'Rational?' Her words fueled his anger further.

He placed a new piece of tape across her mouth.

'I'm going to enjoy this,' he said, taking his knife out of his belt.

Kelly's eyes widened with fear as he wielded the blade in front of her. He inserted the tip under the neckline of her t-shirt, slicing the material to the shoulder, then tearing it with his hands.

'Do you know how to skin an animal?' he asked, looking straight into his prey's eyes.

She shook her head, terrified about what was to come.

'A cut is made from the butt to the lower lip. Then you make similar ones up each leg,' he said calmly, his knife glinting as it caught the light from the greenhouse.

He sliced through the other side of the garment, her ruined clothing falling down. Exposed, vulnerable and tied to the chair, she was powerless to protect herself. Wearing only a sports bra and a pair of shorts, she could feel his eyes studying her semi-naked body. Contempt and disgust marked his face as he breathed hard. Kelly tried to shuffle back to escape him, attempting to put distance between them but she was already up against the wall. Without warning, he slapped her across the face, almost lifting her off the floor. She slumped back, dazed and disorientated. Tony kicked the chair hard, her head clattered into the bulkhead behind her. Sneering, he left, slamming the door behind him.

Unable to lift her head, her breathing had become deep and erratic. In the darkness, she vomited, bile-stained mucus dribbling from her chin onto her chest. Fighting unconsciousness seemed like holding onto sand - the more she fought against the blackness, the more the particles ran through her fingers until the hourglass was empty.

28.

'I hope you don't mind me asking,' said Anna, as they ate breakfast. 'Why are you called Kenwyn?'

'How do you mean?'

'It sounds like a Welsh name, but you come from South Africa?'

'Kenwyn isn't really my name,' the medic said. 'It's the area of Cape Town where I used to live.'

'So, why do you call yourself Kenwyn?'

'My real name is Bokamoso Traore,' he said. 'When I first signed up for the Agency, they mixed up my first name with my place of birth, and the rest is history.'

'That doesn't mean you have to use it.'

'Well, it just seemed like a lot of hassle having to change everything, you know, my email address, my dog tags and so on. So, I became Kenwyn.'

'Bokamoso,' she said, playing with the word in her mouth. 'Don't you mind people not calling you by your name?'

'Not at all. It's where I'm from, and I'm proud of

that.'

'Do you mind if I still call you Kenwyn?'

'Not at all, everyone else does.

They two of them cleaned away their breakfast things, stacking the trays in the rack.

'What can they be doing in there?' he asked rhetorically, gesturing to the sealed door.

'I don't like it,' Anna said. 'It's been far too quiet.'

'Well, it is technically mutiny,' he said. 'They still execute people for that.'

'I hope it doesn't come to that. I'm going outside to see if I can work out what's going on.'

'Do you want me to come with you?' he asked.

'No, I think it'll be better if I go on my own, one of us needs to stay here and make sure they don't shut down the airlock.'

Dressed for going on the surface, she waited impatiently for the light to turn green. Once outside, Anna crept around the perimeter of the dome and the new accommodation block. The greenhouses were constructed from a specially-designed polymer which polarized the low levels of sunlight, maximizing the growing time, but were robust enough to withstand harsh conditions on Mars. She pressed her tinted visor up against the window, peering inside. Through the rows of plants, Tony and Wai were embroiled in a heated discussion. The botanist leant against a shelving unit while the assistant commander ranted at her animatedly. Anna's eyes scoured the long, thin interior of the greenhouse, but there were no signs of Kelly. Unsure whether this was good or bad, Anna increased the brightness of the lights on her helmet, attempting to improve her view. Tony stood with his fists clenched, slightly taller than his conspirator; Wai cowered with her head bowed, diminutive and tremulous. He spotted Anna on the other side of the plexiglass, instantly losing his temper. He released an angry tirade before storming out, the words lost but their intent penetrating beyond the wall. She knocked on the glass, trying to catch Wai's attention, but she looked away, refusing to make eye contact. Anna tried again but was waved away before Wai hurried after Tony.

***

The cabin was small but functional. Peter offered a seat to his guest as if nothing had happened. Mac sat in the chair next to an untidy bed, coming to terms with his current reality. The hooded man placed another chair opposite him then made two cups of coffee. A palpable silence hung in the air; each man afraid to talk. Placing the mugs on a small table, Peter flopped ungainly onto the seat, unable to bend.

'Sorry I hit you earlier,' Mac apologized, breaking the awkwardness.

'I understand,' Peter said, sipping awkwardly at the coffee. 'You must believe me, I meant you no harm.'

'I can see that now. Can you imagine how terrifying it was for me being bound to an operating room bed by a hooded figure?'

The cloaked man nodded, saying nothing.

'Tell me what happened to the rest of the crew,' Mac said.

Peter fidgeted, clearly uncomfortable with the request, 'Ever since the selection process, something clicked, we were close friends. Two of them were killed by the impact when the Erebus crashed. The wall of the cockpit was stoved in, crushing the mission specialist and Joey, the cartographer,' he said reluctantly. 'At that point, I was relatively unhurt, only a few scratches. Although it was damaged, the capsule was still intact, and the air was still breathable. I unfastened my safety belt and managed to pull the commander into the Comms Room. He was severely injured, but still alive. I went back and freed Helen, our system engineer. Her femur was broken, but she was otherwise okay. As I struggled to lift her through the door, the oxygen supply ignited, causing a huge fireball. My uniform caught fire, but I was able to drag her through the door. The pain was immense, but I had to save her. I slammed it shut behind me to stop the fire spreading to the rest of the ship. I had to roll on the floor to extinguish my burning clothes. Hans, our geologist, was still inside the capsule. I had to listen as he died, locked in the cockpit.'

'I'm so sorry,' Mac said. 'I can't imagine what that must have been like.'

'You really don't want to know. I still find sleeping difficult; I can still hear him screaming every night.'

'Helen's lower torso and legs were burnt, too deep and extensive for her to survive. Sadly, she died in my arms shortly afterwards.'

'What happened to your mission commander? You said you were able to get him out.'

'He had sustained significant blunt abdominal trauma during the crash,' Peter said with the matter-of-fact attitude doctors discuss patients. 'His liver was damaged, and he needed surgery to stem the bleeding. I attempted to operate on him, but my hand was so badly burnt. I couldn't hold the instruments properly. He died on my operating table. It was all my fault.'

'You can't blame yourself. You were seriously injured. He would have passed away if you hadn't tried. You were his only hope.'

'It wasn't enough. I buried all of them a couple of weeks later, once my hand had healed.'

'It sounds horrendous,' Mac said empathetically.

'I thought I was going to live out the rest of my life on my own. That's why I wanted to keep you here. I didn't want you to leave me. I'm sorry.'

'Well, you don't have to be, I understand.'

'You're very kind,' Peter smiled, deliberating turning his head, so only the unburnt half of his face showed.

'I need to get back to the Aeolis. They think I'm dead. Why don't you come back with me?'

'I'm not sure whether I can, looking like this. I'm not ready to meet a group of people.'

'They won't mind your appearance,' said Mac. 'And remember, you're officially the first person to walk on Mars. Your name should be in the record books.'

'Let me think about it,' Peter said.

***

The dingy space epitomized her failure, darkness engulfing her. Trapped in the chair, Kelly felt incredibly vulnerable, the hot and humid room becoming increasingly claustrophobic. Slowly, her demons revealed themselves. Fear, loneliness and frustration swirled around her, exacerbating her isolation.

The door swung open. Tony lurched in, smelling strongly of alcohol.

'So, you're awake,' he said irritably.

She said nothing.

'Look at you,' he shouted, staring at her vomit-stained chest. 'You disgust me.'

Kelly sat there helplessly, afraid of what was to come. She watched nervously as her assistant commander removed a pair of pliers from his trouser pocket. Again, he waved them threateningly in front of her face, tormenting her for his own enjoyment. Tony untied her left hand, roughly pinning it to the arm of the chair with his knee. Gripping the fingernail of her index finger in the teeth of the pliers, he squeezed until the nail splintered. Kelly winced, trying to withdraw her hand. Unperturbed by the fear in her eyes, he pulled hard, ripping the nail from its bed, prompting a blood-curdling scream. Throwing down the tool, with the fingernail still trapped between its jaws, he launched menacingly. She shrieked loudly as blood dripped steadily from her hand onto the floor.

'Hurts, doesn't it? But I don't think you've been humiliated enough,' he sneered, forcing his knife under her bra strap, nicking her skin. Kelly stared at him, her eyes desperate and pleading. An expression of victorious satisfaction washed over his face, her muffled screams falling on deaf ears. Reveling in her fear, he began sawing through the dense material, the blade causing the fabric to fray easily.

'Tony!' Wai screamed from the doorway. 'I did not agree to this.'

He stepped back, as the botanist rushed in, positioning herself between him and his victim. Wai gently removed the tape from Kelly's mouth, then unfastened the remaining bindings.

'I'm so sorry, Kelly,' Wai said regretfully. 'Tony persuaded me he wanted to talk to you. Not this.'

Dirty and bloodied, the commander leaned heavily against the botanist as they staggered through the greenhouse, leaving Tony alone in the cell with an uncomfortable realizing he had gone too far as the wave of adrenaline subsided.

'He's not going to hurt you now,' she whispered repeatedly, leading the commander to her cabin before laying her on the bed.

29.

After much deliberation, Peter elected to stay aboard the Erebus. For the first time in many days, Mac slipped on his exosuit, relieved to be wearing the uncomfortable protective outfit once again.

'I'll come back for you,' he said.

'I need to get my head around it all', Peter said. 'It'll be a big step, you know, meeting other people.'

'Take your time. Everyone will understand, it will take a while for you to adjust.'

Waiting for the airlock to decompress, Mac stared through the window at his unfamiliar surroundings. It looked similar in its rocky barrenness to the Gusev crater, but the mountains were more precipitous.

Once outside, he descended to the surface, stepping back and surveying the wreckage. The deformed, charred ruins of the capsule dominated this end of the ship. Mac couldn't believe anyone could survive that level of destruction. The starboard side of the spacecraft's fuselage was also extensively damaged, but the other remained relatively intact with only slight cosmetic damage, summing up Peter's tenuous existence.

Two Rovers were parked neatly at the foot of the steps, one from the Aeolis, the other presumably from the Erebus. It must have taken him hours to ferry them back and forth, so they were now both here. He identified his vehicle; the cab was a slightly different shape, and it bore red flashes on the side which were absent from the other. Once inside, he pressurized the cabin, watching the slow-moving gauge until it gave a satisfactory reading. Placing his helmet on the passenger seat, he pressed the ignition button. The engine burst into life, filling him with childlike excitement. He swiftly programmed the Rover's navigation computer then set off in search of the dome.

He could not remember the journey during the storm, his memories either too hazy or lost. Although what had transpired was clearly disturbing, Mac had to admit, he would have died if it was not for Peter's timely intervention. The Rover trundled through the alien landscape, throwing up clouds of red dust as he made his way across the mountainous plains. Mac's mind flashed back to the maelstrom which had engulfed him, causing his pulse to race and bringing him out in a cold sweat.

The vehicle entered the Valles Marineris, an extensive series of canyons scarring the planet as far as the horizon. After a couple of hours of travelling, he turned off, following the computer, ascending a steep incline onto the plain of Tharsis, a vast, rocky plateau near the Martian equator. A few feathery clouds drifted in the yellow sky above him. In front stood three enormous shield volcanoes with giant

Olympus Mons looming menacingly in the distance. He came to a stop, donned his helmet then stepped outside.

Turning around slowly, Mac took in the panorama of the planet's western hemisphere. The landscape was alien, yet strangely compelling. He exhaled heavily, partially misting his visor while marveling at the beautiful scenery around him. A warm feeling rose inside him; he was alive.

From his elevated position, he looked back down the valley. The beauty was breath-taking. Although it had only been a short period of time, Mars had got under his skin. Standing for some time, deep in reflection, he found peace within himself. Mac knew he belonged here.

***

Sitting beside the commander's bed, a knot of anxiety weighed heavily on Wai. She spoke calming words in Cantonese, attempting to settle Kelly's troubled dreams. She had slept throughout the night, and Wai had never left her side. What had happened was so far removed from what she had envisaged, it now caused her immense pain and a heavy burden of shame. Dampening a cloth in a white bowl, she began wiping at the dried blood in Kelly's hairline. Wai dabbed the wound on her cheek, causing Kelly to stir. Despite closing it with adhesive strips, Wai was sure it would leave a scar. A permanent reminder of her treachery, apparent for everyone to see.

Tony appeared in the doorway, 'How is she?' he

asked sheepishly.

'Not good,' she replied. 'Can you unlock the door? I need Kenwyn to take a look at her.'

'I only wanted to make her listen,' he tried to explain.

'No, Tony,' she said curtly. 'You were trying to break her.'

30.

As the sun set, the Rover moved onto familiar ground, lumbering over the uneven ground, past the site where Mac had discovered water. After a very long journey, he could finally see the dome in the distance. He parked outside then decompressed the airlock.

Hearing the airlock depressurizing, Kenwyn rushed from the kitchen and stared through the corridor window. Confused, as he knew everyone was inside. His first thought was perhaps Kelly had escaped, but from the shape of the body, it was clearly a man, and it was certainly not Tony.

The airlock seemed to take an age to re-pressurize before the person in the airlock removed their helmet.

'Mac?' Kenwyn mouthed through the glass.

Mac grinned at him, placed his helmet on the rack, then unzipped his exosuit, letting it hang at his waist. He opened the internal door and stepped into the corridor.

'We thought you were dead,' Kenwyn said finally,

embracing his colleague.

'It's a long story,' Mac replied. 'Let's sit down with the crew, and I'll tell you about it.'

Mac followed the medic into the Dining Room, where Anna was eating a bowl of reconstituted pasta. The color drained from her face as he entered the room.

'How?' was all she could say.

'Hi Anna,' Mac greeted her with a smile.

'I didn't think I'd ever see you again,' she said, leaping up and throwing her arms around him.

'I missed you too,' Mac said. 'Where are the others?'

Anna looked furtively at Kenwyn.

'What?' Mac said, sensing something was amiss.

'Things have changed a little while you've been away,' the medic said reluctantly.

Kenwyn and Anna explained the events since his disappearance. Mac's face becoming furrowed as he listened.

'Do you think my disappearance tipped Tony over the edge?' he asked.

'I don't know,' said Kenwyn. 'I think it was a culmination of things. Perhaps losing you in the storm was the straw which broke the camel's back.'

Mac sat in silence, slowly absorbing what had been said.

***

Wai remained at Kelly's side, watching her sleep restlessly. A few hours previously, Kelly had woken briefly but quickly drifted off again. Wai was relieved Kelly was okay but knew the repercussions of the last few days were going to haunt her for some time. Suddenly, a voice crackled over the dome's intercom.

'Attention all crew,' a familiar voice said. 'This is Michael MacDonald. I am not dead. Come and join me in the Ops Room,'

'What?' exclaimed Wai, assuming it was some kind of sick joke.

Disbelieving, Wai left her seat and walked down the corridor to the locked door. She peered through the glass, attempting to see if this was an elaborate hoax. To her surprise, Mac was sitting on Kelly's desk, waving at her through the glass. Tony shuffled along the corridor behind her, not believing what he had heard.

Mac leapt to his feet, pressing his face against the glass.

'It's okay Tony, it's me,' Mac said reassuringly.

'I don't believe it,' Tony muttered, tears welling in his eyes.

'It's true,' Mac replied. 'Why don't you come through and we can talk.'

Tony tapped the access code into the control pad and opened the door. He cautiously walked into the room and threw his arms around Mac, sobbing uncontrollably.

'You're alive,' the assistant commander said, wiping tears from his cheeks. 'How did you survive?'

'It'll take a lot more than a storm to finish me off,' Mac said jovially. 'Let's have a coffee, and I'll tell you all about it.'

'Before that,' Wai interrupted. 'Can you take a look at Kelly?'

'Sure,' said Kenwyn nervously. 'What's happened?'

As they walked along the corridor, Wai explained how things had got out of hand and that Tony had assaulted Kelly. On entering the room, Kenwyn knelt alongside his commander, quickly assessing her. Most concerning was Kelly's reduced level of consciousness.

'I need to get her to the Infirmary,' Kenwyn said grimly. 'I need to run some tests.'

He slid his arms under Kelly's limp body and carried her. She snuggled into him, not aware of what was happening. The medic walked cautiously along the narrow corridor towards the medical facility. All the time, Wai followed, observing nervously.

Kenwyn laid her down on the assessment bed. He quickly connected her to devices which measured her vital signs. He listed to her chest with his stethoscope then connected her to a cardiac monitor. Worried Kelly was dehydrated, Kenwyn connected up an intravenous line and gave her a slow infusion of fluid. Next, he checked her blood sugar, but thankfully it was normal. He removed a pen torch from his top pocket and shone it in her eyes, holding each eyelid open in turn with his thumb.

'How is she?' Wai asked.

'I think she may have a traumatic brain injury,' the medic said sternly.

'How bad is it?' Wai asked, dreading the worst.

'I won't know until she's had a scan,' he said. 'But we don't have the necessary equipment here.'

'What are we going to do?'

'There's not a lot we can do, other than wait and

hope.'

'Thank you,' Wai said sincerely. 'I'll sit with her if you want to go and see Mac.'

***

Kenwyn re-joined the others in the Dining Room. Mac, ever the colorful raconteur, was holding court while the others sat around him listening intently.

'How is she?' Mac asked, noticing the medic enter the room.

'I'm not sure,' he said candidly. 'I need to run a few tests. Wai's sitting with her.'

His words forced Tony to look away.

'Anyhow, tell us what happened to you,' said Kenwyn.

'Well,' Mac said, instantly returning to storytelling mode. 'When the storm hit, I managed to make it to the Rover. I tried to drive back to the dome, but none of the instruments were working, and I couldn't see anything. So I had to sit it out.'

'You've been in the Rover all this time?' Anna asked incredulously. 'That's not possible. The air would have run out long ago.'

'No, my oxygen reserves were virtually zero, and I started to drift in and out of consciousness. I thought I was going to die.'

'So, how did you survive?' Tony interrupted.

'I was rescued,' said Mac casually.

'Rescued?' Kenwyn repeated, looking at the others. 'By who?'

'We're not alone on the planet,' Mac said with a

mysterious air in his voice.

'Shut up,' the medic recoiled. 'You're not going to tell me you were saved by little green men.'

'Not quite, but we weren't the first people to walk on Mars. Disappointingly, I'm not even the first person to drive here.'

'You're not making any sense,' said Anna.

'I was saved by Peter McCarthy.'

'Who's Peter McCarthy?' Tony asked, somewhat puzzled.

'Wait,' said Kenwyn. 'I remember that name. Wasn't he on the Erebus?'

'Exactly,' Mac said. 'He took me back to the crash site. He found me in the nick of time.'

Mac explained about Peter's horrific injuries and what happened to the rest of the crew. A million questions were thrown at him, and he dealt with them individually. A ping from an incoming call interrupted the conversation. Kenwyn hurried to the Operations Room, closing the door behind him. It was from Ryan. The medic reluctantly opened the message, revealing the deck of the Discovery.

'Hi,' Ryan said. 'How's the situation down there?'

'Things have taken a couple of unexpected twists over the last few hours.'

'How so?' he asked nervously.

Kenwyn described Mac's miraculous return, finding a survivor on the Erebus, then Kelly's health issues.

'So, things have de-escalated?'

'Yes, apparently, Wai talked some sense into Tony, and Mac showing up really helped to break the deadlock.'

'How's Kelly now?'

'Not good,' the medic said. 'She's in the infirmary. I'm worried she may have a traumatic brain injury.'

'How bad is it?'

'I honestly have no idea.'

'Hang on,' Ryan said anxiously. 'I'm patching in our Chief Medical Officer.'

The screen flickered momentarily before a second face appeared alongside the commander of the Discovery.

'Can you see us okay?' Ryan asked.

'Yes,' he answered.

'Kenwyn, this is Dr Jose Vasquez, our CMO.'

'Yes, we know each other. We trained together at the Agency.'

'Hi Kenwyn,' the Mexican physician said. 'It's good to see you again. How is life on Mars?'

'I'm fine, thanks. It sounds like you've had an eventful journey.'

'Not one I'd like to relive if I'm honest.'

'Okay, I'm not sure how much Ryan has told you, but things have been a little taxing down here too. I need your help. Our commander has sustained a head injury. She's rousable, but a little confused. I'm not worried about an intracranial hemorrhage, but I can't be certain of the extent of any underlying brain damage. I don't have the necessary equipment to scan her down here.'

'We have a small MRI coil on the Discovery,' Jose said. 'It's not able to image torsos, but it can do heads and single limbs.'

'Perfect,' Kenwyn said.

'The Agency said we're not allowed on the planet surface until the quarantine period is up,' said Ryan. 'That ends at midnight. I don't want to land in darkness unless I really have to. Is she well enough to wait until tomorrow?'

'I think so,' said Kenwyn. 'If she deteriorates, I'll contact you.'

'Okay,' Ryan said, clearly unsettled. 'Thanks. Jose, can you make sure you're ready to receive them as soon as we land.'

'Of course,' he said. 'We'll be waiting for you in the morning.'

With that, Jose's face disappeared, Ryan's image now occupying the whole screen again.

'How's the atmosphere in the dome?' he asked, once he was sure Jose had left the communication.

'Slightly better now Mac is here.'

'Who's in command down there?'

'Technically, Tony is while Kelly is incapacitated, but I don't think he's mentally fit.'

'It doesn't sound like it,' Ryan observed. 'I'll take control when I land tomorrow. In the meantime, keep an eye on things, but don't be too obvious. We can't risk antagonizing him any further. If there are any problems, you can always get in touch.'

'Thanks,' he said before ending the call.

'What was the message?' Anna asked as he entered the room.

'The Discovery lands first thing tomorrow.'

Tony eyed him suspiciously, knowing the medic would have discussed the events of the previous days with Kelly's husband.

'We need to prepare for the imminent arrival of considerably more personnel on the planet,' Kenwyn said.

'But the accommodation block isn't completely finished,' Anna said. 'The wiring in there is still a little basic.'

'I wouldn't worry; many hands make light work. With all the extra people, it will be completed in no time.'

31.

The Infirmary was quiet; only the subtle hum of the condenser was audible. The hands on the clock hanging opposite Wai were moving slowly as she flicked through the pages on her tablet, catching up with news back on Earth. A few hours remained before she could hand over to Kenwyn and get some sleep. Beside her, Kelly let out a grunt. Looking up from the text on her screen, Wai watched as the commander's body became tense and her limbs contracted; her face twisted into a snarl. Kelly began thrashing around uncontrollably, her arms and legs convulsing rhythmically and her lips turning blue, froth gathering at the corners of her mouth. Terrified, Wai slammed the alarm button on the wall, immediately setting off a siren which echoed around the whole dome. Seconds seemed like hours before Kenwyn dashed in, pushing past her and kneeling next to the bed. Talking tenderly, he placed an oxygen mask on Kelly, put a hand on her shoulder and observed.

'Can't you give her something to make it stop?' Wai asked, distraught and tearful.

'I'm hoping it settles on its own,' the medic said, drawing up some gloopy, colorless fluid from a vial.

Kenwyn glanced at the clock, praying the convulsion would subside, but it continued unabated, and beads of perspiration began to collect on the commander's forehead. Grudgingly, he tapped the syringe on the edge of the worktop to remove any bubbles, then squeezed out the remaining air. He injected the contents into the intravenous cannula residing in the crook of her arm and waited. After several long minutes, the beats of Kelly's limbs slowed.

She lay unrousable, her breathing labored and deep. Letting out a sigh of relief, the medic shone his pen torch into her eyes, watching her sluggish pupils react. Next, he increased the sedation in an attempt to suppress any further seizure activity.

'Is she alright?'

'I think so. She'll just need to sleep it off. Maybe you should do the same.'

'Will you call me if anything happens?'

'Of course, but I've turned up her sedation, so I don't anticipate any changes for the next few hours.'

'Thanks,' Wai said before trudging towards her quarters.

Thankfully, there had been no further seizures, but as the drugs wore off, Kelly began mumbling agitatedly. Kenwyn attempted to talk to her, but the conversation was one-sided and nonsensical, her answers unrelated to any of his questions.

Later, wearing just a medical gown, she tried to sit

up.

'I'm okay,' she said. 'Leave me alone.'

'I need to examine you,' he said patiently. 'There are things I have to do.'

'Well, can you turn the lights down? Kelly asked. 'It's a bit bright in here.'

He adjusted the setting, so the room's main light was off, leaving on only those peripheral lights above the work surface.

'Is that any better?' he asked, but she did not reply. 'Do you remember how you hit your head?'

'Yes, I.... I banged it on the stairs,' she confabulated.

Kenwyn smiled knowingly as she filled in the gaps in her memory with fabricated answers.

The door slid open with a screech, causing Kelly to throw her hands up to her ears.

'It's okay. You're a little more sensitive to noise because you've had a bang on the head.'

Anna popped her head in, 'How's the patient doing?'

'I'm fine,' Kelly said. 'I've been telling him, but he's not listening.'

'Tony took a message from the Discovery,' Anna said. They're about to begin their descent.'

'Tony? I bet that was awkward,' said Kenwyn.

Kelly tried to stand up.

'Where are you going?' he asked.

'We can't let them in,' said Kelly. 'They'll start touching things.'

'What do you mean?' the medic said.

She continued to struggle to her feet, agitated and distant, straining the lines and cables attaching her to the various monitors.

'Hang on. Let me disconnect you first.'

***

The crew stood in the corridor watching through the window, Kelly fidgeting restlessly, her mind clearly elsewhere. It had taken Kenwyn some time to persuade her she was not well enough to venture onto the planet surface to greet them. According to protocol, Tony had assumed command while she was incapacitated, but the rest of them had an uneasy anticipation as he put on his exosuit in the airlock.

They could hear the Discovery long before they saw it, Mac the first to spot the massive ship on its final approach. Considerably bigger than the Aeolis, it hovered momentarily, the giant engines throwing up vast clouds, obscuring its descent.

The ground shuddered as it touched down. From the safety of the corridor, the rest of the crew watched as ant-like figures descended to the surface. Tony slipped on his helmet then depressurized the room in preparation for their arrival. Four people hurried across the rocky ground before entering the dome.

He attempted to shake Ryan's hand as the room re-pressurized, but the Discovery's commander ignored the gesture. Once the light turned green, everyone removed their helmets.

'I would like to welcome you to Mars,' Tony said, holding out his hand again.

'Tony Zaragosi, you are under arrest for the crime of mutiny,' Ryan said formally. 'You have the right to remain silent. Anything you say can, and will, be used against you in a military tribunal. An attorney will be provided for you.'

'What do you mean? There's surely been some mistake,' Tony objected.

Ryan nodded to his sergeant-at-arms, the tall woman with severe features standing beside him. She stepped forward, gripping Tony forcibly around the wrist. In one swift movement, she had positioned him with his face against the wall, his wrists handcuffed behind his back.

The sergeant nodded at Ryan.

'Thank you,' he said.

Next, he opened the door leading to the small corridor where the rest of the Aeolis' crew were standing.

'Wai Xu, you are under arrest for the crime of mutiny,' said Ryan, repeating her rights.

She said nothing, her shoulders visibly sagging as the color drained from her face. Reluctantly, she held her hands out in front of her, but the sergeant-at-arms wrenched them behind her back before securing them.

'A court-martial will be arranged for a convenient date, and your case will be heard,' Ryan said before Wai and Tony were frog-marched away.

Ryan approached Kelly with a beaming smile. She looked at him awkwardly, unsure who he was. To break the awkward silence, she led the way to the Ops Room.

'I'm sorry you had to witness that,' he said. 'How are you feeling?'

'Not too bad,' she said, unclear why he was interested.

'We need to get you ready for an MRI,' Kenwyn said.

'I don't need a scan,' she protested. 'There's nothing wrong with me. I'm just tired.'

'I'll be the judge of that. Now, can you put your exosuit on please?'

'There's no need for any fuss,' she grumbled.

In the airlock, the medic and Ryan watched as she struggled to dress in her suit. Putting her arms in first instead of her legs, she tried to step into her exosuit, unable to comprehend why she could not get dressed. Ryan had to help her, finally fastening it at the front for her. He attempted to kiss her on the cheek, but she shrugged him off.

Fully suited, they made the short journey to the Discovery. Once aboard, they were hurried to the ship's Medical Bay where Dr Jose Vasquez was waiting for them.

'Hi, Jose,' Kenwyn said, shaking his hand.

'Good to see you again,' the Chief Medical Officer replied. 'And you must be Kelly.'

'Yes,' she said. 'I don't know why they've brought me here.'

'Apparently, you've had a nasty blow to your head, and Kenwyn wants to make sure everything is as it should be.'

'It'll be fine,' she said dismissively, distracted by the sight of the MRI scanner through the window.

'Great, let's do a quick scan so we'll all be happy.'

Wearing nothing but a gown, Kelly was led into the Scanner Room and laid on a flat trolley. A technician positioned her head, using a grey foam block for support. Jose made her cross her arms on her chest, as if she was an Egyptian mummy, then placed tight bands around her, preventing her from moving.

Jose joined Kenwyn and Ryan in the control room where they watched her through the glass.

'The table's going to move in a moment. Try and stay as still as you can,' Jose said, pressing a button on the console, opening the microphone.

The trolley began to inch horizontally, moving Kelly's head into the ring-shaped scanner. Over the space of twenty minutes, several grainy, monochrome images appeared in front of them.

'There's the problem,' said Jose, scrolling through the screens.

'What is it?' Ryan asked, trying hard to hide the worried inflexion in his voice.

'It's a contusion in her right frontal lobe,' Jose said.

'Sorry I don't understand. What does that mean?'

'That part of the brain is bruised,' said Kenwyn, pointing at the screen with a pen. 'It explains her symptoms. These lobes are responsible for memory and personality.'

'Will she get better?' Ryan looked desperately at the two medics.

'This kind of injury usually takes several weeks to resolve, but even after that, she may continue to have residual problems.' the Discovery's CMO said. 'There's no way of knowing how badly the brain has been damaged until the bruising has settled.'

'You mean she could always be like this?' he exclaimed.

'It's unlikely she will remain as bad as this,' Kenwyn said. 'It's still early days. She'll improve over the next few months, but we don't know by how much.'

32.

Despite having driven this route numerous times before, Mac followed the Rover's onboard computer closely. Having his commander sitting next to him made him nervous.

'How have you found taking over from Kelly?' he asked.

'It's similar to commanding the Discovery, mostly politics and managing people.'

'If you don't mind me asking, how's the boss doing? It's terrible what happened to her. I feel guilty for the part my disappearance played in causing this.'

'No one holds you responsible, and thankfully, she's on the mend. Her memory is improving, but she still has some word-finding difficulties. The biggest problem is poor concentration. She get's so frustrated.'

'What does Kenwyn think?'

'He's happy with her progress. He thinks she'll make a full recovery. I'm quite nervous about meeting Peter,' Ryan said, changing the subject.

'Oh, he's a nice guy, but understandably, he's a bit messed up after the crash.'

'I think all of us would be if we'd experienced the things he has.'

The Rover ascended onto the plateau where the remains of the Erebus littered the rocky ground.

'Look at that,' Ryan exclaimed, studying the wreckage.

'Yep, it's a miracle anyone walked out alive. Anyway, we're here,' Mac said, pulling up next to the ruined ship.

Slipping on their helmets, the two men climbed the bent strut towards the airlock door.

'Peter,' Mac shouted after re-pressurization. 'Are you in?'

'Yes,' a voice came from one of the rooms. 'I'll be there in a second.'

'How has this place survived?' Ryan whispered, surveying what remained of the spacecraft.

'For what do I owe this pleasure?' Peter said, coming out of his quarters, quickly adjusting his hood to hide his scars.

'Peter, may I introduce you to Commander Ryan Brown,' the Scotsman said. 'Commander, this is Dr Peter McCarthy.'

'It's an honor to meet the first person to walk on Mars,' Ryan said.

'Thanks, Commander,' the Erebus' medic replied. 'Unfortunately, it wasn't the momentous experience you'd imagine.'

'Yes, I hear things were a little rough.'

He ushered his visitors into one of the side rooms

off the corridor, showing Ryan to a chair then rushing out to find one for Mac.

'How have you been?' Mac asked as their host sat down.

'Good thanks,' he shrugged. 'There's always something I can find to do around here. Oh! While I remember, commander, I would like to thank you for the supplies you allowed Mac to bring on his last trip over here. It made a refreshing change to add some variation to my diet.'

'You're very welcome,' said Ryan. 'That brings me to what I wanted to talk to you about. I was wondering whether you'd like to move into the Aeolis Base with the rest of us. We have a room ready for you in our residential block, and we would love for you to come and join our community.'

'I've been expecting this,' Peter said, shifting uncomfortably. 'Won't people be put off by my appearance?'

'Not at all,' Mac said. 'You're a bit of a legend back at the dome.'

Peter fidgeting nervously with his hood.

'I would like our medical teams to examine your burns,' Ryan added. 'I suspect they could help.'

'It will be fine,' Mac reassured his friend. 'Everyone wants to meet you.'

Peter looked at them for reassurance.

'Okay,' he said finally. 'I've thought about this ever since the Aeolis landed, and, if you're sure it wouldn't be an imposition, I'd be delighted to.'

After being shown to his new quarters and a guided tour of the facility, the colonists held a party to mark their arrival and welcome their newest member. The ground floor of the accommodation block had been hastily decorated, and a small spread of food had been placed on a table against the wall. Daunted by meeting a large number of people, Peter wore his black hood over a clean flight suit, his right hand gloved as usual. Despite feeling a little like an exhibit at a freakshow, he was welcomed with open arms. However, he could not help noticing a little friction between the original crew of the Aeolis and those who had recently arrived.

Kelly found the crowd too much, her senses addled by the sensory onslaught. She loitered near the door, spending most of the time watching from the corridor.

'Here you are,' said Ryan. 'How are you bearing up?'

'There's so much noise, I can't think straight.'

'You're doing fine,' he said, putting his arm around her waist. 'It's bound to be overwhelming while you're recovering,'

'I guess so,' she said. 'How did your call go with the Agency.'

'They asked how your recovery was going,' he said softly. 'They also want Tony and Wai moved from the Discovery to the Erebus,'

'I suspected as much, but it'll mean the security guards will have to travel long distances between shifts.'

'There are not really any other options. Even with the residential block, there's no space in the dome to house them securely.'

'I suppose not. Can we skip the party? It's giving me a headache.'

'I have to make a speech, you know, officially welcoming Peter to Aeolis Base. Why don't you go and lie down? I'll come and find you as soon as I'm free.'

***

The expansion phase of the colonization had started in earnest. Cramped and frenetic, it had become a hive of activity, with every available inch of floor space becoming occupied by crates and pallets, crammed full of supplies from Earth.

After overseeing the construction of the additional floors of the residential block, Ryan managed the colonists' transition from living on the Discovery to inhabiting the new buildings at Aeolis Base.

The goal now was to accelerate the agricultural program, making the colony self-sufficient within five years. With Wai incarcerated, a botanist from the Discovery, Dr Marko Heikkinen, had taken over the food production program. Currently, trials of new wheat hybrids were underway, using the seeds from the most successful plants the Aeolis' botanist had grown. Alongside these, the greenhouse now housed hundreds of tree saplings in preparation for the following year's terraforming project, once the giant solar mirrors had been deployed to melt the polar ice.

'How are you?' Ryan asked as he snuck into the darkened room.

'Much the same,' Kelly said, 'it's so frustrating.'

'Don't worry, you're clearly better than when I first arrived, just slower than you would like.

'You're late coming back,' she said. 'Is the party still going on?'

'I left when Mac started singing. Anyway, I had a meeting,' he said, slipping on a fresh t-shirt. 'The Agency have decided the trial will be conducted offline. I guess they don't want a public spectacle.'

'It's damage limitation,' she commented, tripping over her words. 'Our exploits have harmed the organization's reputation. Do you know how the whole thing is going to work?'

'Apparently, testimonies and submissions are going to be considered by a panel of three senior military officers on Earth.'

'Have they said which ones?'

'I don't think they've decided.'

'I hope we get someone friendly. Have they given any indication of how we're going to provide statements?'

'Video recordings, I guess.'

'So, how will the cross-examination happen?' she asked, clearly anxious about the process.

'They're going to send us questions once they've reviewed everything. It's the only way they can manage the time delay. When there are no loose ends to tie up, they'll adjourn to deliberate.'

'Then we'll have a long wait.'

'I'm not sure,' Ryan admitted. 'The evidence is quite overwhelming. The Agency have said they will broadcast their verdict to Mars before making it public back on Earth.'

Kelly thought for a while. 'That's fair. Tony and Wai should be told before the rest of the world. But it all feels unsatisfactory.'

'A little, but I'm glad I don't have to go face-to-face with a military defense lawyer.'

'Giving evidence against members of my own crew will be unpleasant, however I do it.'

***

Under the bright lights of the Infirmary, Jose and Kenwyn scrutinized Peter's injuries.

'What was your field of expertise?' Jose asked, making polite conversation while he probed the extensive area of scaring on Peter's right arm.

'I was a cardiologist before joining the Agency,' Peter explained self-consciously. 'Heart rhythm disorders were my special interest.'

'I was a plastic surgeon,' Jose said, turning his attention to his badly burnt face. 'It seems horrible to say, but I enjoy operating on injuries like this. I find it rewarding. How about you, Kenwyn? What was your specialty?'

'Trauma and Orthopedics. I like nothing better than sticking metalwork on a broken bone.'

'Right, I'm done,' said Jose, removing his gloves. 'There's a lot we can do here. Where the skin has scarred, it has tightened. The majority of your symptoms, like the restriction of your right shoulder, are from these contractures. My plan is to release these by making incisions across the points of maximum tension, then closing them with a split-skin graft. That should improve the range of movement, free up your neck and allow you to close your mouth.'

'Do you think it will heal?' Peter asked.

'I think so,' said Jose. 'Your skin will never be

entirely normal, but we can reduce the scaring and restore some of the function.'

'Where will you harvest the grafts from?' Kenwyn inquired.

'Well, we haven't got many options, due to the extent of the injuries, so I will have to take them from your left thigh and buttock.'

Peter started sniggering.

'What's so funny?' the surgeon asked, somewhat puzzled.

'When I meet people, the first thing they'll see is my ass.'

Jose tried to suppress a laugh while typing his notes.

'The biggest decision I have to make is whether to do one long procedure or tackle your shoulder separately,' he said, trying to get the conversation back on track.

'If you did that, which would you do first?' Kenwyn asked.

'I would like to do the head and neck first,' Jose said. 'As they seem to be causing you the most problem, but I'm tempted to do it all at once. What do you think, Peter?'

'If you can do it all in one sitting, then I would rather that.'

'It would mean a long anesthetic time, which would carry more risk.'

'I understand, but the way I see it, I have nothing to lose.'

'Okay,' said Jose. 'Should we do it tomorrow?'

'That soon?' Peter said anxiously. 'It all seems a little quick.'

'You've had these scars for two years. There's no

reason to wait any longer.'

33.

'How are you?' Kenwyn asked, sitting on the counter in the Infirmary.

'Okay,' Kelly replied. 'I'm still getting headaches, but my concentration's improving.'

'How about your fine motor skills, like buttoning a shirt?'

'No problems.'

'Good, how are things between you and Ryan?'

'How do you mean?'

'You didn't recognize him when he arrived.'

'I don't remember the Discovery landing at all,' she said, her face saddening. 'It's all a bit of a blur, but everything's fine now. I feel so guilty about what I put him through.'

Kenwyn carried out many psychometric tests, assessing her mood, sequencing and decision-making skills. At the end he deemed her fit to retake command.

'Ryan to the Infirmary,' he said into the intercom.

A few moments later, Kelly's husband burst through the doors, flushed and out of breath.

'What is it?' he said, his eyes flitting between the medic and his wife.

'Sorry, I didn't mean to panic you,' Kenwyn said. 'I wanted to give you some good news. Kelly is well enough to retake command.'

'That's great news,' Ryan said, still trying to regain his composure.

In the corridor, Ryan and Kelly chatted readily, with no formal ceremony announcing the transition of power, only a brief conversation sealed with a kiss.

Kelly's next task was to record her testimony to supplement the statement she had written a couple of days previously. Her recollection of the events was cloudy, she could only remember Tony's outbursts following Mac's disappearance and little else. Her legal counsel had advised her to admit that there were things she did not remember rather than attempting to fill in the blanks.

One of the security guards stood in front of the Dining Room door. He stepped to one side as Kelly approached, allowing her to enter. Kenwyn sat at one of the benches. He had already recorded his statement and was waiting for further questions to come back from Earth. Dark patches stained his underarms, and his skin glistened with perspiration. For the first time, she noticed the medic looked exhausted, his usually unflappable persona clearly ruffled by a grilling from the lawyers.

'Well, this is an unpleasant return to duty,' she said, pacing back and forth anxiously.

'I know. I was in there for over an hour. I want this whole wretched debacle to be over.'

'How did it go?'

'Draining,' Kenwyn admitted. 'I thought I'd covered everything in my statement, but there were hundreds of difficult questions.'

'What did they ask?' she said, lowering her voice.

'Primarily, they wanted to know about your leadership before the mutiny, then a lot of stuff about Tony's mental health and the extent of your injuries. They had some doctor as an expert witness asking lots of medical questions.'

Her heart sank.

'Don't worry,' he said quickly, seeing the anxiety appear on her face. 'All I did was tell the truth.'

'I know you would have, but it's all very stressful.'

'We now have to wait for the message to be sent to Earth. The panel will review it and decide if they want to ask anything else.'

The Discovery's sergeant-at-arms, who had facilitated the recording of Kenwyn's testimony, appeared in the doorway to the Ops room.

'You can relax,' she said, looking at Kenwyn. 'They have no more questions for you. Commander, you're next.'

Kelly rose from her seat and began walking slowly towards the intimidating woman.

'Good luck,' the medic said.

'Thanks,' she said, without looking back.

***

The time had come for the Discovery to return to Earth, another momentous milestone for the fledgling colony. The unmanned ship would soon begin its slow homeward trudge, scheduled to take a few months longer than the outward journey due to them being at the end of the launch window. Similar to the ill-fated Aeolis, all usable equipment had been stripped from its interior. Walking wistfully through the corridors, Ryan relived moments from their eventful trip; some memorable, like celebrating the successful Mars landing and some he would rather forget, like the Hantavirus outbreak and dealing with the deaths of several of the colonists. On the bridge, he sat in his chair one last time, soaking in the eerie atmosphere, before accessing the NavCom for the return journey. He clicked the interface, programming the launch to begin in an hour. A series of automated announcements began, playing over the intercom systems of both the Discovery and the dome, warning everyone of the impending departure and to steer clear of the ship.

The announcement interrupted Kelly giving evidence, the recording having to be paused and restarted several times before she was finished. Then, she sat with the sergeant-at-arms as they reviewed the footage to make sure they were happy with it, making sense there was nothing else she wanted to add. Seeing herself on the big screen, describing the events of the days leading up to her kidnapping, made her feel inadequate. Next, came a list of questions which had been sent by the lawyers working on behalf of Tony and Wai.

'Commander Brown, is the apparent breakdown in discipline due to your failure as a leader?' a stern-looking lawyer said on the video screen.

Kelly fumbled her way through an answer, but it felt unsatisfactory.

'Commander Brown, I put it to you, that your handling of the disappearance of Michael MacDonald triggered your crew's lack of faith in you and your ability to successfully execute your duties.'

'Not at all,' she insisted. 'Mac was unfortunate to be on the surface in the storm. None of us saw it coming. It happened so fast. He was just in the wrong place at the wrong time. I was not prepared to put the lives of any of my other crew at risk to search for him while conditions were so bad.'

The hostile inquiry continued, becoming increasingly harder as the questions progressed.

After a slow and laborious, but still intimidating, cross-examination, Kelly was requested to wait in the Dining Room while the lawyers and panel members worked through the available evidence. To her surprise, Ryan was sitting on one of the benches, waiting for her.

'How was it?' he asked, giving her a hug.

'Tough. There are too many things I can't remember.'

'They'll understand.'

'Apparently, Tony and Wai recorded their statements yesterday,' she said. 'The lawyers made it sound as if it was my fault.'

'They're trying to triangulate what you're saying with the testimonies of the others, that's all.'

'You should have heard the lawyers' questions,' Kelly said. 'They essentially accused me of being responsible for Mac's disappearance.'

'Don't worry, they're just doing what lawyers do.'

***

Kenwyn injected the colorless contents of a plastic syringe into Peter's left arm before securing his airway. The ventilator began pumping a mixture of air laced with additional oxygen into the patient's lungs while he lay unconscious. Checking the blood pressure and confirming the infusion pumps were running at the correct rate, Kenwyn nodded to Jose. It was safe to proceed.

Wearing a gown, gloves and a mask, Jose and his similarly attired assistant placed sterile drapes over their patient before cleansing the surgical site with iodine. He was the kind of surgeon who worked in total silence, with only the ventilator and the resolute beep of the oximeter disturbing the tranquillity of the Operating Room. Kenwyn sat back, anticipating a long afternoon of measuring vital signs, as Jose put knife to skin.

The procedure lasted several hours. Jose only stopped for a comfort break and a quick coffee. At the end of the surgery, Kenwyn wheeled the trolley Peter was lying on into the Recovery Room where he could be monitored during the post-operative period.

'Are you happy?' Jose asked, his mask pulled low, his eyes exhausted.

'Yes,' Kenwyn said. 'His blood pressure's been fine throughout, and now he's breathing spontaneously.'

'Excellent. Peter's going to be a bit sore when he wakes up, so make sure he has plenty of opiates on board.'

'I'll keep him asleep overnight and wake him up tomorrow.'

34.

The ground shook as the engines of the Discovery came to life. Kelly and Ryan watched from the dome's airlock as the spacecraft lifted from the rocky surface, hovering momentarily before the giant vehicle started its homeward journey.

'Well, we're on our own for the next two years,' she said.

'Strange feeling, isn't it?' he commented after pausing for a few seconds.

'What?'

'Knowing we're stuck here and can't leave, even if we wanted to.'

She nodded, her gaze not moving from the surface.

'I'm not sure about any of it anymore,' she said finally.

'How do you mean?'

'You know, being responsible for all this,' she said down-heartedly. 'After everything that's happened, I don't feel cut out to run this place.'

'You can do it,' Ryan said, taking her hand. 'What happened was not your fault. No matter what had gone on before, Tony's actions can never be justifiable.'

'I hope the Agency see it that way.'

Anna opened the door behind them, the screech of metal on metal making them jump.

'They've reached a verdict,' she said, her voice a mixture of excitement and fear. 'They're transmitting it via a video message in around three hours.'

'Thanks, Anna,' said Ryan as she disappeared.

'That didn't take long,' Kelly said. 'It must be bad news.'

'You're over-thinking,' he said patiently. 'It doesn't mean anything. Anyway, we need to get ready.'

The security guards aboard the Erebus had been notified and were already heading back to Aeolis Base with the prisoners. After all that had happened, Kelly really didn't relish the thought of being in the same room as Tony and Wai again.

Despite Mars being one hundred and forty million miles from Earth, there was going to be a colossal amount of interest in the trial's outcome. Kelly had received regular updates from friends and family back home in her personal messages. Even the proceedings in the Ops Room were being filmed. Being on the front pages of every newspaper and media broadcast was mortifying, particularly for something which questioned her ability to command. Knowing she was to be the focus of the world's press, Kelly changed into her formal uniform which she had last worn at Mac's unnecessary funeral. At least, if outwardly she appeared professional, it might help sway the public's perception of her, whatever the verdict.

A buzz of nervous energy filled the Ops Room with every square inch occupied by people jostling to see the announcement. The crowd spilt into the Dining Room and along the airlock corridor, everyone desperate to see the defendants. Immaculately dressed, the commander and her husband fought their way through the throng of people, heading for their reserved seats in the front row on the left. Before they could sit down, the intimidating sergeant-at-arms bellowed an order, prompting everyone to stand.

'Here we go,' Ryan whispered. 'Good luck.'

Kelly looked straight ahead, stony-faced, oblivious to everything else around her.

The two prisoners marched in, flanked by security guards. Both of them stared down, avoiding eye contact as they took their places on the other side of the aisle from her and Ryan. After a few moments, the giant screen flickered to life. The auditorium of the Agency appeared, looking solemn and far removed from the euphoria of their launch celebration. Three stern-looking, high-ranking military officers, representing the Americas, Europe and Asia, accompanied by the chairman, sat behind a long desk draped with the Agency's insignia: their posture severe and unforgiving.

Kelly stood bolt upright, her uniform cap clasped tightly under her arm. The chairman banged a gavel on the table, rising to his feet, 'This tribunal has assessed the evidence relating to the failed coup d 'état at Aeolis Base, Mars. It has been a unique experience assessing this case remotely. Nonetheless, we ensured due process was followed, and counsel, have had the opportunity to review the facts and cross-examine the witnesses and the accused. You may be seated.'

Those lucky enough to have a seat, sat down while the European General on the screen rose and stood behind a podium, pausing dramatically even though this was a pre-recorded message.

'Could the prisoners please stand,' he said, clearing his throat. 'Assistant Commander Anthony Benjamin Zaragosi. For the crime of mutiny and assault of a senior officer, you have been found guilty.'

Tony paled as the gravity of the verdict hit him.

'The punishment for such an offence is typically death by hanging. However, the panel felt there were extenuating circumstances. According to your medical officer, Dr Kenwyn Traore, the grief associated with the suspected demise of your friend and colleague, Lieutenant Michael MacDonald, affected your mental health and clouded your judgement. Consequently, this tribunal sentences you to thirty year's incarceration. March him out.'

The two guards flanking Tony turned simultaneously before the three of them marched out.

'Thank goodness he wasn't sentenced to death,' Kelly muttered to Ryan as a photographer captured her response to the outcome of the trial.

'Professor Wai Xu,' the General said ominously, reading from a card. 'For the crime of mutiny and the assault of a senior officer, you have been found not guilty.'

The botanist dropped to her knees, tears rolling freely down her cheeks.

'On reviewing the evidence, we believe you were misled by one of your superior officers. You may return to active service with immediate effect. March her out.'

Her two escorts hoisted the diminutive botanist back to her feet, then turned and quick-marched from the room accompanied by excited chatter which had erupted around them.

'How do you feel?' Ryan asked his wife, trying to make himself heard above the noise.

'It's hard to describe. I'm pleased for Wai but sad for Tony. It's going to be tough on him.'

'Yeah, it all seems such a waste, and keeping him locked up when we have such a small population is going to be a drain on resources, not to mention losing his construction expertise.'

'We should keep him on the Erebus,' Kelly said. 'He can't go anywhere from there without a Rover. I think we can continue to benefit from his skills, but he will be housed away from the rest of us.'

'That seems fair, but you'll need to post guards to supervise him. That will use up personnel who, otherwise, could be helping with the building.'

'I know. It'll have to be one-to-one supervision. That'll reduce the impact on the remainder of the colony.'

***

A nurse was plotting vital signs on a computer when Kenwyn returned to the Infirmary.

'How's the patient?' he asked, washing his hands.

'Okay, I think. His vitals are stable,' she said. 'But his urine output tailed off a little, so I increased the rate of his drip. I hope that was the right thing to do?'

'Yes, that's perfect,' he said, glancing at the screen over her shoulder. 'And I think we can stop the sedation. Let's wake him up and see how he feels.'

Over the next few minutes, the drugs wore off. The endotracheal tube soon irritated his throat, causing Peter to gag as his conscious level improved. Deflating its cuff, the medic removed the life-saving device, dragging stringy strands of mucus with it.

Within a quarter of an hour, the patient was sitting up, still a little groggy, but fully awake.

'How are you feeling?'

'A little sore.' Peter's voice sounding croaky and wet.

'Do you need any pain relief?'

'I'm okay for the moment, thanks.'

Kenwyn walked over to the intercom on the wall. 'Dr Vasquez, to the Infirmary please.'

Sometime later, Jose strolled in and glanced at Kenwyn before his eyes settled on Peter.

'Time to take off these bandages,' the surgeon said, carefully unwrapping the bandage around Peter's head.

The results were impressive. A lot of the scar tissue had been removed. His mouth now closed without the fixed grimace, and his neck movements were much improved. Jose held up a mirror for Peter to review the results of his surgical handiwork. His face appeared raw and angry, but the extensive injuries were gone, replaced by a healing skin graft.

'Thank you,' the patient said, his voice breaking with emotion as he studied his reflection. 'It looks better than I had expected.'

'It will continue to improve over the next few weeks,' said the surgeon. 'I'm afraid I couldn't save your right eye, but I have this for you.'

Jose handed him a black, elasticated eyepatch, 'Don't put it on yet. The skin needs to heal some more first, but once everything calms down, this should come in useful.'

Greasy dressings were reapplied to the burns by the nurse, who then began wrapping fresh bandages around them before allowing Peter to sleep.

'Hi Kenwyn,' Kelly said with a smile, sliding open the Infirmary's door. 'How's our patient doing?'

'Come and meet him,' the medic replied. 'He's just finished his breakfast.'

He led her through to the two-bedded room off the main assessment area. Peter struggled to sit up on seeing his visitors.

'Hello,' she said. 'I'm Kelly Brown, the commander of Aeolis Base.'

'It's a pleasure to meet you, Ma'am.'

'Kenwyn tells me your wounds are healing well. I do hope he's looking after you.'

'I've received fabulous service,' Peter smiled. 'Everyone has been so lovely.'

'You're welcome. When you're better, I'd like to pick your brains and get your opinion on a few things.'

'That's kind of you. I'm not sure I can contribute much though. Not with my injuries.'

'You survived on your own on this planet for two years. You're obviously a resourceful man and the colony would benefit from your experience.'

'Thank you,' Peter said, unaccustomed to the attention. 'I would love to help in any way I can.'

'I'm putting together a leadership committee to ensure all the decisions made are the right ones. When you've recovered, I was wondering whether you would like to be part of it.'

A smile broke over the patient's face. 'I would be delighted to.'

Within days, the Erebus' medic had been discharged from the Infirmary. Peter struggled into the wheelchair, and the nurse placed his cloak across his knees. Mac wheeled him along the corridor towards his new quarters which had been furnished by the Scotsman with the few belongings Peter had left on the wrecked ship.

'Here you go,' Mac said, as they entered the room.

'It looks lovely,' Peter said, taking in the new decorations.

'Is there anything I can do for you?' he asked, fussing over him.

'There is one thing.'

'What do you think?' Mac asked, looking in the mirror over his friend's shoulder. 'You're almost unrecognizable from the man I met back on the Erebus. Fewer scars and now a shaved head.'

'It's going to take some getting used to,' Peter said, studying the face staring back at him, exploring his bare scalp with his fingers. 'I want to thank you for everything you've done for me,' he said formally. 'And I'd like to apologize for how I treated you when we first met.'

'Let's not worry about that. We just got off on the wrong foot, that's all. You have a whole new life to look forward to now.'

Over the next few months, Peter grew in confidence. The hooded cloak had been abandoned in preference for a burgundy baseball cap. He continued to wear the black glove on his disfigured right hand, but now sported the eyepatch Jose had given him. He had become a bit of a celebrity amongst the other colonists.

***

Kelly knocked reluctantly on the door, not wanting to have this conversation. After a few moments, the door opened slowly. Wai peered at her uncomfortably, her eyes betraying the shame she tried to hide.

'Please, come in,' the botanist said in little more than a whisper.

The commander entered the small room, closing the door behind her. A parchment containing traditional Chinese script hung on the wall above a solitary saucer on a small, wooden table, bearing a tired-looking red apple and a serrated knife.

'How are you?' Kelly asked, trying to work out the symbolism of the odd arrangement of ornaments.

'Okay,' Wai said, her tone withdrawn and labored.

'I thought it was best we cleared the air. First, I want to say thank you for saving me. I hate to think what would have happened if you hadn't intervened.'

'He said he only wanted to talk to you,' said Wai, tears brimming in her eyes. 'You have to believe me. I had no idea what he was planning.'

They sat in silence for a few awkward moments before Kelly spoke again, 'I'm so glad the court-martial found you not guilty. You didn't deserve what he put you through.'

'It was so stressful,' she said, wiping her tears away with a tissue. 'Every action was scrutinized by security guards.'

'Let's talk about how we move forward,' Kelly nodded.

'What do you have in mind?'

'I want you to continue your work developing radiation-resistant cereals,' she stated. 'Before all this happened, you were making some significant advances.'

'That would be great. I'm told the new hybrids are just germinating.'

'However,' Kelly said forcibly. 'I don't think it's appropriate for you to continue to lead the agricultural program. I'm going to ask Marko Heikkinen, from the Discovery, to take charge. From now on, you will report to him.'

Wai nodded solemnly, breaking eye contact. 'He's a very able botanist,' she finally mumbled, her voice quivering.

'Good,' said Kelly, standing up. 'I thought we should have this chat so we can move forward.'

'Thank you,' Wai said quietly.

Kelly smiled then left.

Ryan was waiting for her in the airlock as the two suns were setting. Kelly put her arm around his waist, and he squeezed her across the shoulders. Comfortable in each other's company, they stood silently until the distant sun disappeared behind the Columbia Hills

Made in the USA
Coppell, TX
19 September 2021

62686717R00152